High praise to a powerful new author!

"Being a writer of traditional westerns, I couldn't imagine what the combination of vampires and cowboys could be like. Well, I just finished Colin Webster's book and now I know. Solid, never ending action with a twist at every corner. A refreshing change, I must say."

– Will Riley Hinton
Author of "Lonely are the Hunted" –

"Colin has done something that is very rare, and very special these days. He's written a good Western that you can sink your teeth into like a nice thick beef steak seared over the open flame of a camp fire. You can smell the desert sage and feel the grit carried by the wind and it makes you squint your eyes as you read. But this isn't your Dad's Western, some surprise elements are going to grab you. By the time you finish the book, you'll be wearing a cartridge loop belt to work. This is a great story and I am eagerly looking forward to the sequel.."

– George Hill
Author of "Uprising USA" and "Uprising UK"–

"*Blood and Tequila* doesn't just bend the mold of a traditional western, it shatters it. Great characters combine with a fast-paced plot to form a solid debut novel. And, c'mon. Cowboys and vampires--vampires and cowboys. This ain't your pappy's Saturday afternoon read!."

– Josh Clark
Author of "The McGurney Chronicles" and "Dakota Divided" –

"In Colin Webster's book, *Blood and Tequila*, the author has done something I didn't think was possible. Skillfully, he has managed to blend two conflicting genres, the Western and Sci-Fi. With Webster's strange but riveting mixure of cowboys and vampires, perhaps the book should have been called, The Quick and the Undead."

– RG Yoho
Author of "Death Comes to Redhawk" –

"Cowboys and vampires, what a combination, and Colin Webster does it with flair. *Blood and Tequila* is a rip-roaring read. This book is just plain fun."

– JK Jones
Author of "In Due Time" –

Acknowledgements

I would like to thank the folks at White Feather Press for making this happen and helping Clay and Maria come to life with excellent design, editing, and story input, and the excellent group of fellow writers at wethearmed.com for all their encouragement and criticism.

COLIN WEBSTER

Blood and Tequila II:

Blood on the Mississippi

Published by White Feather Press, LLC
www.whitefeatherpress.com

ISBN: 978-1-61808-055-4

Printed in the United States of America

Cover design created by Ron Bell of AdVision Design Group (www.advisiondesigngroup.com)

White Feather Press

Reaffirming Faith in God, Family, and Country!

This book is dedicated to
my mother, Pamela Webster,
for everything that she does for me and
for teaching me how to read and enjoy
books at an early age. Without that, it
would be awfully hard to write them!

CHAPTER 1

The Vampiress came at me, fangs bared. She was dressed all in white, moving so fast she looked like a ghost. She'd been just waiting to ambush me. I'd followed her trail here, thinking it was easier than it should have been to find her. Too easy. Maybe I shouldn't have wandered into the graveyard. But then, I'm Clay Wilder, and I go where others fear to tread

I spun and whirled somehow, just fast enough so that her claws merely tore my new store bought shirt to shreds. That made me mad. My attacker's momentum carried her far past me, and before she could turn I filled my hands with wood and steel and fire.

I cut loose with both guns, but she was already gone, my .44 slugs screaming off headstones.

I crouched low and moved behind a granite slab, my guns to either side. My eyes cast about vainly trying to penetrate the thick shadows under the low hanging willows. She was out there still, somewhere.

There! Behind a tall stone vault, a trace of wrinkled white cloth could be seen peaking out the side. She gave too much away, wearing white like that. You'd think a creature of the night would dress in something dark and gossamer, or some other such material. I moved low and slow, on cat feet, slinkin' and a'slidin' my way through the gravestones right up to the edge of the vault. I had her now.

Easing back the hammers of the six guns, I took a deep breath and whirled around the corner.

I grinned, ready to empty my guns into...an empty white dress.

"Looking for someone?"

I turned, but it was already too late. A small but iron-hard fist drove into my chest, knocking me sprawling into the dirt. I came to rest wrongside up, my head stopped my tumble against cold, hard marble. I tried to raise my guns but my hands were empty, stars swirled in my vision.

The vampiress swept in, smooth and graceful, you'd think she floated. Her cruel, exquisite lips twisted up at the corners, revealing a small, sharp set of pearly fangs. She had me, dead to rights.

Her soft black hair brushed my face as those fangs grew closer and closer. Instinctively I drew my neck back as far into my shirt as I could, like a turtle...only less effective.

Her lips met mine the next instant, and I forgot about my hurts, and near everything else, for a moment.

"You made it too easy." Maria whispered, a note of reproach in her silken voice.

"You didn't play me fair. 'Sides gal, it's awful hard for any man to draw a bead on his own wife. Though I'm told if you give it a few years, its gets easier and easier."

Maria laughed at that. I climbed painfully to my feet, found my hat and stuffed it down over my ears. She was getting better.

We hadn't stayed long in Rio De Sangre, The order Maria's brother belonged to, the late Father Cortez, had showed up in force only a few days after we'd burned out the tunnels under the village, cleansing the town of the monstrosity buried under it for hundreds of years. The three of them were hard, dangerous looking men, looking more apt to stick a knife in you than turn the other cheek. I suppose their line of work called for a different kind of priest. The order of Saint Michael, they called themselves. Named after the good Lord's warrior angel. They might have worn collars of white, but they didn't seem like the kind of folks even a gunslinger like me wanted to tangle with. Still, I'm Clay Wilder, and around me everything tends to get wilder and wilder. It was no different this time.

We'd asked them to marry us, since Miguel was dead and gone, but they would have none of it. They were downright suspicious of us, and when we heard them preaching to the villagers about the need to finish the cleansing of the town, we knew better than to stick around and find out what they'd meant. I'd dug up Maria while she slumbered the day away and loaded her onto the back of a wagon, as the sun disappeared behind the horizon; we rode hard, my steeldust making hay for the border. The northern one this time. Hadn't ever had to run for that one before. My trusty steed had come tearing out of the remains of the tunnel shortly after I'd seen Maria rise from the grave for the very first time. I wasn't entirely sure how that happened, but I figured him going down in that tangle of vamps must've changed him somehow.

Even with a vampiric steed pulling the wagon, the priests of the order had caught up to us. As fast as he was, the wagon would have been tore to bits had he run as fast as he was able. The priests must have been trying to catch up to us afore Maria had the chance to rise. She hadn't been eating, other than what I could spare her from my own supply, and was weakening. It had been taking her longer by the day to rise back to life. I took it as a sign she was starving.

The priests caught up without much trouble. They started throwing lead, a posse of villagers strung out behind them, carrying torches, and not just for the light they gave. Guess they decided Maria was a threat after all, an unholy creature what needed cleansing from the earth.

I argued with them the best way I knew how, which is to say I let my Winchester do the talking. My arguments were short but loud and to the point, and they backed off after two of them went down. We'd been running from them ever since.

First we went west, but there was no hiding from them. The territory was too open, too much risk of getting caught by day; and Maria was awfully vulnerable in that big pine box. Even with the steeldust's vampiric speed, they would always be waiting for us, only a day or two behind.

So we turned east. I still had a good portion of that shipment of gold, though I regretted leaving most of it for the ungrateful villagers who'd turned on us. We'd landed on the Mississippi, spending our days going up and down the river. We'd even found a barefoot preacher at a church in the woods to get us hitched up right and proper-like. Of course we didn't tell him about Maria's condition, though he did think it a bit odd what with us insisting on a night time wedding. I don't know if that was legal and all, in the Lord's eyes, but we both said the words and meant them. I guess it was new territory. Vampire or not, she was still a gal and I was still a feller, and just because she would still be young and fresh as a daisy while I'd be old and wrinkled and gray one day, didn't seem like it should nix the deal, though that fact has been on my mind more'n once in the past few months.

They caught up to us at Natchez, ducking out of an alleyway with pistols. Maria leapt in front of me, and soaked up most of the lead. I gunned down one, but the other got away with only a bullet in the hindquarters for his trouble. Served him right. Maria healed quickly, but her thirst grew more, and it was all she could do to keep from draining someone dry right there. She tried to stay away from folks, and I searched out other ways to get her the nutriment she required.

Since then we moved every day. Maria bedded down in a different place, we'd been using steamboats to move up and down the river at random. While Maria slept, I tried my hand at cards and other games, and managed to increase our small fortune somewhat.

We'd been practicing, me playin' the part of demon hunter or whatever you'd call it, and Maria playin' the part of, well...Maria. Graveyards was at least private and secluded, and oddly enough they was the one part of Memphis where you wasn't in danger from choking to death from the smell of manure and garbage.

"Your ah, dress seems to have gone missing darlin'." I stammered out, my eyes a little busier than my brain.

"It's just over there."

"Are you uh, goin' to be puttin' it back on?"

"Not just yet." Maria flowed to me, her eyes and figure full of promise.

"We're in a bone yard darlin', don't you think-"

"I'm tired of thinking. Of worrying about the next few hours. Of being on the run. You promised to love and cherish me Clay. We haven't had much time for that. There's a nice soft patch of grass over there, and it doesn't look like anyone's lying there. Maybe we should."

"That's kind of dark, isn't it?" One part of my brain was a little hesitant to do my marital duties in a graveyard, another part of me was telling my brain to just shut up and get on with the loving and cherishing bit.

Maria's lips twisted into a wry grin, showing a hint of fang.

"I am a creature of the night after all. What's the matter Clay, worried I'll steal your innocence?"

Well, that tore it.

"Gal, a body can't steal what's long been gone. You just bring yourself over here, and-"

"Die, unholy minions of darkness!"

They came running out of the trees. At least five of them. The nearest one threw a jar of holy water, which broke on a headstone and splashed all over Maria's exposed skin. Instead of the terrible screaming I'd expected, all we heard was a Spanish gal's howl of rage. She was madder'n a wet hen, only twice as wet. I suppose her not bein' evil and all made her immune to the effects of the sacramental liquid, though the order wasn't likely to be convinced.

These men might think they were on a mission from God,

5

but in my book they were just tryin' to kill us. They threw water, I threw back lead. My Colt Thunderers lit up the darkened graves as I dealt death like cards, and two of the hooded figures fell.

A man in a black robe came at me from the shadows, swinging a flashing sword. Something pale and blurry smashed into him and he was knocked flying behind a head-stone carved like an angel. Maria zipped over to her dress, and had it on in less than a second.

I snapped shots in all directions, but they closed in on me with axes and swords raised high. After so much prac-tice with Maria moving at speed, the men seemed slow and clumsy by comparison. I ducked a blow from an axe and smashed my knuckles into a hooded face. Dodging to the side, I spent my last bullet poking two neat holes in a robe and whatever was underneath it. They just kept coming. More and more robed and hooded figures appeared from the shadows with blades of all kinds. They boxed me in and closed in a rush. I braced for the first cut that would slice me wide open. Next thing I knew Maria had me in her arms and was off and running, leaping the tall fence around the cemetery without even breaking her stride.

We ran well into the woods, stopping only when we reached the edge of the Mississippi. In the lights from the riverboats cruising on the water, Maria and I checked each other over for wounds. She'd taken a bad cut to her thigh and another to her back, probably when she'd dove into the mass of swinging blades to rescue me. They were already healing.

I wasn't much the worse for wear, exceptin' a black rage that washed over me soon as I knew Maria was safe.

"Clay, what are you doing?"

I was already stalking off back to the graveyard, stuffing shells into my Thunderers.

"I'm finishing this, once and for all. They caught us by surprise, but now it's time for some payback. They've got wounded, so they won't be able to just melt away like they've done before. If'n I don't find them at the cemetery, I'll check the doctors' offices around town."

"You're not going without me." Maria crossed her arms and glared.

I almost told her where she could go, I was that mad. But over Maria's shoulder the horizon was already brightening. The dawn.

"We've got to get you in the ground."

Maria blew a strand of raven hair from her eyes. She was beautiful when she was angry. She was beautiful always.

"It's too far from the last spot, and they might know where that is. I don't know how they've been tracking us, but we've got to get away from here. I don't want them finding me in the daylight, or you, alone."

I holstered my guns and hitched up my belt.

"I got along just fine by my lonesome for quite some years afore I had a vampire bride, lookin' after me. You just dig in, and I'll be here. Don't forget to call that nag before you bed down. Who knows where he's got off to."

Maria put her fingers to her lips and whistled. I couldn't hear a thing, the pitch was too high, but in less than a minute the steeldust came crashing through the trees, his muzzle dripping blood.

"At least he's fed," Maria pouted.

And there would be a very confused cowpoke or horseman somewhere, wondering how his mount had come to be a shriveled husk, drained dry outside a tavern. The steeldust had cleaned out an entire stable outside of Vicksburg less than a fornight past, after a long run. We'd planned on staying a while and resting up, but instead I'd left a hundred dollars and we'd moved on up the river.

While I'd been reminiscing, Maria'd dug a pit big enough for her and the horse together.

The steeldust whinnied and let himself fall over into the pit, for all appearances dead. The first few times I'd had to

7

distract him while Maria broke a log over his noggin until he'd gotten used to the idea of sleeping in the ground. Despite my mood, I had to chuckle at the memory.

Maria yawned and stretched. The sun was about to start coming over the horizon.

"Goodnight, my love." She kissed me deeply, once, and walked gracefully down into the earth. Folding her arms over her chest in a position of repose, she closed her eyes and died for the day.

I hurried to shove the huge mound of earth she left into the pit. Kicking the rest of the dirt into the hole as best I could, I then began gathering fallen branches and leaves and logs, trying to cover the churned earth to make it look halfway natural. The result wasn't very good.

I built a smoke and stood about for a moment, watching the sun rise. Normally I'd watch over her, but it was occurring to me more and more that sooner or later there'd be nowhere left to run. We'd made it this far, and I was tired of running. It was time to take the fight to them.

The priests hadn't attacked during daylight in the whole time since we was chased out of Rio De Sangre, though I didn't know why. I doubted they'd change things up now. I hitched up my gun belt and stalked off through the woods. Today, I'd get me some answers.

CHAPTER 2

Revenge is a dish best served after a hearty breakfast. I'd been spending most of my time between Maria at night and gambling what was left of my ill-gotten gains during the day. That left me skipping more meals than I should have without really meaning to. My ribs was beginning to show, so I tucked into a plate of bacon, eggs and biscuits like a starving man. Pushing back from the table, I loosened my belt a few fresh cut notches and left two dollars on the table.

The stench of the city was botherin' me less and less, but I was learning to ignore it, the way a fella' out on the trail got used to his own smell, which got awful bad after a month of ridin' under the sun in the same set of clothes. I wondered how Maria could stand to be around me of a time.

Building a smoke, I moseyed on down the streets of Memphis. First, I needed a change of dress. Maria teased me that I still dressed like, well in her words, "a saddle-sore cow-puncher with exceptionally poor taste for his class." There was all types along the Mississippi, folks from east and west and north and south all mixin' in together and blendin', sometimes not so well. Bein' that I was a feller what needed to blend in a little better than I did, I went huntin' for a new set of duds.

I stopped and looked myself over in the window outside Jarman's Gentlemen's finery and sundry store. I was raw-boned and lean, my face still burned dark by years of sun and wind, despite the fact that I'd been spending most of my time in smoky gaming rooms on steamboats or prowling the darkness alongside my bride. Even with the heavy breakfast in my belly, I was looking a mite too lean, though my shoulders appeared even wider by contrast. My long dusty rider's jacket covered the torn yellow and black checked shirt I wore over denim trousers and scuffed riding boots.

Perhaps my appearance was why I'd had some early success at cards and other games on the riverboats, most of the gamblers would see me as an easy mark, a traveling cowpoke long from home, pockets full of money, ignorant of their slick ways. At least not more'n one or two feller's had tried to rob me, my rough looks combined with the fact it didn't look like I carried a small fortune in a bellyband under my shirt made for a good disguise.

Now perhaps, it was time for something different. Blending in among the gambling set might afford greater opportunity, there were some more exclusive sets in town putting up high stakes on small hopes, who could afford to be liberated of some of their excess liquidity. I was learnin' me all kinds of new words out here. I didn't figure it would hurt none to clean myself up for Maria neither, a fella as hard on the eyes as I am needs all the help he can get.

I took a deep breath, summoned my courage and pushed my way into the store.

"Welcome to Jarman's Gentlemen's finery and sundries! May I help you Sir?"

A small thin man, impeccably dressed, approached me. He smelled like petunias.

"Yes, I'm here for the uh...some finery and such." I managed, my eyes crawling over the racks and shelves of fancy suit coats and crisp white shirts. I swallowed hard.

"May I suggest this for you?" The dapper little man sang, holding up a gray jacket and trousers. It wasn't none too fancy, perhaps it would serve.

Five minutes later I was standing in front of four different mirrors, the little man marking up my perfectly good suit here and there with chalk. I couldn't figure out why they'd sell such things if there was that much on 'em what needed fixing, but there it was.

"There we are sir, just a few minutes and we'll make those alterations, you'll be the talk of the town in your new suit from Jarman's, oh yes." The man called back over his shoulder as he left me in my underbritches, taking my new clothes back to fix whatever he thought was wrong with them. I frowned, and built a smoke. I didn't want to be the talk of the town; I was trying to blend in with the other riverboat slicks. My plan was already backfirin', and it wasn't even noon.

As I stood there feelin' a mite sheepish in my longjohns, hat, and boots, two men entered the store; a little bell at the entrance rang merrily.

"Clerk is in the back, he'll be out directly," I offered helpfully.

"Just a moment gentlemen, I'll be right with you!" The clerk's voice rang in out in that quavering singsong tone of his. Lord knows what he was doing to my perfectly good set of duds back there. I hoped it wasn't anything out of the ordinary.

The two men who'd entered ignored me and fanned about the store, looking all over. The hairs on the back of my neck stood on end. They wore regular store bought clothes, some of the creases still in them from the shelf. They didn't look interested in buying any "finery", but then I didn't either. But something about them was off, I couldn't put my finger on it. My gunbelt was wrapped up at the foot of the mirror, my Derringer was tucked in my boot. I'd managed to find a two shot model in .41 down in Vicksburg, the better to match my revolvers. That ace in the hole had saved my hide more'n once.

The two men spread out in the store, their eyes moving but not really looking at anything. Then their eyes swept to me. I didn't have any doubts what was about to happen. When their eyes went hard I knew the ball had opened. It was time to ante up.

11

As one, they reached down into waistbands and the next thing I knew two bright flashes of metal whistled through the air at me. I ducked down and the mirror behind me shattered into a thousand pieces. Fetching the Derringer out of my boot, I popped up behind a rack of coats and snapped off two shots, but the men were already ducking and moving behind the other racks. Ante in.

One of the men dove over the counter as I snatched up my guns. The second hurled another knife which buried itself in the floor an inch in front of my head.

"Oh my goodness gracious!" The clerk appeared at the back of the store and shrieked, his hands fluttering.

The man behind the counter popped up and smashed the butt of a double barreled shotgun upside the clerks head, he dropped like a stone.

My eyes went wide as the shotgun leveled with my head. I popped back down like a prairie dog into the maze of suits and racks of ties as both barrels went off and the rest of the mirrors shattered. I shrugged off the shards that covered my shoulders and landed in my hair, and moved as quietly as I could to the side, my ears ringing. The glass crunched under my feet, it was everywhere. I could only hope the other fellers would have been deafened by the blast.

Through the ringing, I could hear the shotgun break open. He was reloading. No telling where the other one went. I didn't dare peek up to give them another target. If I couldn't go high, I would go low. Crawling on my belly I snaked through the ends of trousers and sleeves on the floor.

On the ground next to me, something moved. My nerves must have been strung high, since I almost put a bullet in it right there. A shard of mirror, showing a knife, a hand, and a leg. But where was the reflection coming from?

A step, a crunch of glass. I turned and fired, right through a pile of starched shirts, and sidestepped. Call.

A groan told me I'd hit something, and I moved low and quiet to the back of the store. Peeking through a wooden rack of dress shoes, I saw the one with the shotgun trying to injun' up on the spot where I'd last fired from.

Easing back the hammer, I drew a bead right between his shoulder blades. His ears perked up, and he threw himself to the side just as the gun bucked in my hand.

I rose, firing after him, and he ran like a rabbit. I managed to wreak holy havoc on all manner of gentlemen's finery but not much else.

Something crashed into me, hard. The man I'd shot bulled me over a low table covered in gloves and watches, and I crashed on my back. My gun went spinning off somewhere, but I still held the belt with the other one in my hand. My attacker rose up, producing a long cruel knife from somewhere, and brought it down hard. I crossed the belt with my hands and brought it up to block the blow at his wrist. He put both hands on the blade and drove down with all his strength, but I'm a sturdy critter, and I managed to hold him off.

That knife hovered there, right over my eyeball. Beyond it, the man's face drew up in a grin. He dropped the knife. I twisted to the left like a bucking bronco, and the blade stuck in the wood inches from my head.

I managed to get one leg up and hooked a boot 'round my attacker's throat, bringing him down to the floor with me, where my fists were waiting. I straddled him and started punching away, in seconds his face looked more like the breakfast I'd eaten this morning than a man.

Something made me look up, and those twin barrels stared back at me again. I rolled right, and the man I'd been pummeling screamed, "NO!".

The man with the shotgun cut loose, but I was no longer there. His partner was. Blood spattered my face and hair, but I was already rising, snatching my second revolver out of the gunbelt.

The man with the shotgun froze, caught in the middle of plucking the empty shells out. He dropped the shotgun, and slowly raised his hands. Fold.

He might be empty handed now, but the murder was still in his eyes. If the situation were reversed, I knew he'd gun me down in a heartbeat. It didn't feel good, but there was only one thing to do.

"Sorry friend, this is one game where when you're in, you're in to the finish."

I drew back the hammer on the Colt. The man sprang for me, another knife suddenly in his hand. I pulled the trigger, but just heard a metal snap instead of a boom. That was bad.

He brought the knife in low, and then thrust upward towards my ribs. I slashed down with my left hand, catching his arm at the bicep, and then thrust the barrel forward into his face. He gave a short sharp URK sound as the barrel popped through his eyes socket, and I let him fall, his feet beating out a tattoo on the ground as he gave up the ghost.

Figuring I'd wore out my welcome at Jarman's, I picked up the suit of clothes and hurriedly dressed. I threw off my old scuffed up boots and swapped them for a pair of finely tooled black ones, and stuffed a wad of dollars in the clerks pocket while he still lay unconscious. After a look at the two bodies and shot up clothing, broken mirrors, and blood spattered furniture, I bent down and stuffed another wad in there.

Leaving out the back door, I buckled on my guns and walked up the next street, reloading as I went.

I made it that far before I remembered the thunderer's failure, and sneered in disgust as I looked the gun over. One of the leaf springs might have snapped and bound up in the works, but it wasn't important. I'd spent more time than I'd cared to breaking the guns down to the last little piece every time I'd fired them, they gummed up something fierce and needed more care and attention than I cared to have to give. I'd always kept my guns clean and ready, but these gals were downright finicky. It was time for something else.

Just so happens, Fogerty's general store had a sign proclaiming the arrival in the latest in what they called "shootery", so I moseyed on in and took a gander.

There was three other fellas looking over the handguns, rifles and shotguns lining the glass cases all along the store. A brightly painted sign called attention to the 1881 model of Smith and Wesson's top break. They were coming out in .44 now, checked hard rubber grips. A minute later I was handling it, but still casting an eye back to a pair of peacemakers in the same caliber. I ended up holding them both. The old reliable or the march of progress? I favored the speedy reloading of the Smiths, I'd no doubt have need of it, perhaps this very afternoon, since trouble was hot on my heels. I'd been looking for it and it was looking for me. On the other hand the Colts felt familiar in my palms, the hammers were easy to find, my thumbs practically itched for them. I was taking a liking to the Smiths just the same, but I was concerned they'd be as finicky and fragile as my last pair of doubles.

In the end I took them both, the Smiths fit the holsters better, and the Colts went under my jacket, tucked through the belt at the small of my back. I'd swapped the derringer out as well, and continued my walk, five guns on my person. The Colts rode easy, I'd taken the ones with three-inch barrels. Most of the riverboats frowned upon going armed at the tables, though many a gambler had a hideout or two, it was bad form to show it brazenly.

It would have been ideal to have a chance to question my attackers. The order of Saint Michael didn't seem to have much trouble tracking me down, but I hadn't much of a clue where to find them. I'd almost rushed back to Maria's grave as soon as I left Jarman's, but if they had known where she was, they would have doubtless rushed us as soon as she went to ground. Apparently they were willing to attack during the day, since they'd just gave it a darn good try this very morning. There was a piece of the puzzle there I didn't have, but it might mean something. They must have had men in town, watching. They'd followed me to the store. They might be following me even now.

I didn't figure they'd make it easy to track them down. A secretive lot they were, I didn't have much hope of finding the hole they'd be hiding in. I could stop at the doctor's offices and make discreet inquiries, but if they had used the services of a sawbones in town, they'd be long gone by now.

Frustrated by that line of reckoning, I took a seat on a bench under an overhang and built a smoke. A carriage rolled down the street pulled by stout horses. An elderly couple dressed in some of that there "finery" strolled down the street under the shade of the old gal's parasol. A few men loafed outside a restaurant, digesting the noonday meal.

Those hairs on the back of my neck stood up again. I was being watched. It was just a feeling, probably a natural one for a man who'd spent his life on the run, and a lot of that lately. I leaned back, puffing the cigarette and trying to look deep in thought, but my eyes cast about discreetly, searching. There was no one out of place, no one that didn't belong there. No rifle barrels glinted from windows, no one lurked in the faint shadows of alleyways.

Still, from my own experience, I've come to believe there are other senses, one which the learned fellers at the universities know little, if anything, about. A body knows when someone's eyeballin' him from behind, particular if that feller has some kind of ill intent.

I didn't know who and I didn't know how, but if the priests were watching me, I'd best stay far away from Maria. I'd have to shake them before sundown, Maria needed to feed. Another thought occurred to me. Why was I wearing out my noggin trying to figure out how to find those who were tryin' to find me? We both wanted the same thing, just with different results.

Grinding out the smoke with the toe of my fancy new boot, I stalked off down the street with a purpose. I wasn't going nowheres in particular, but I wanted them to think I was.

I was a watchful man, by nature and long experience, but I didn't see hide nor hair of them before they'd caught up to me in Jarman's, nor did I see sign of them now. That needed to change. I needed to draw them out. Turning it over in my mind, I figured I needed to force them out, to hurry to keep up with me, but without letting on that I knew they were there. If they sensed I was on to their game they might either pull back, or just get a lot more careful. I had to make it look natural.

Stopping suddenly, I asked a passerby how to get to the waterfront. I knew it was to my left, and that's exactly where I wanted him to point. As he helpfully pointed right down the alley I wanted to go, I tipped my hat and strode off, walking fast. Whoever was following me couldn't hear what was said, I reckoned, but would gather I was going in that direction. They would not know my destination, so they'd have to move quickly to catch up and get ahead of me before I reached the street on the other side.

I walked into the alley, but as soon as I was around the corner, I broke into a run. Slowing to a walk just as I reached the street on the other side, I peered around the corner. Two men came out of alleyways down the street to my left, dressed like regular folks, store bought clothes just like the ones this morning. I suppose it would have been easier for me if they'd worn their Roman collars.

One man strode easily up the street towards me; the other pulled out a newspaper and leaned against some railing. I waited a moment and strode easily out into the street, as if I didn't have a care in the world. I headed for the outskirts of town, to the rough district along the waterfront.

That's right fellas, come and get me.

CHAPTER 3

It was still early in the afternoon, and the crowds of roughs, toughs, and no-accounts grew thick as flies along the waterfront. High falutin' classy steamboats docked alongside rusty hulks as they took on and spewed forth a torrent of humanity in all manner of dress. Seein' so many folks a'comin and a'goin' was still enough to make my head swim. I kept an eye on the one I knew for sure was following me as long as I could, but it wasn't long before I lost sight of him in the throng. So many fellers was giving me the stink-eye I couldn't rely on trying to sniff out who was paying me too much attention. I just kept walking, knowing they were there, counting on it.

Most of the crowds was transitory folk, stopping in while passing through. The yellow fever outbreaks that happened every year for the last few had left entire quarters of the city abandoned, and the sheer amount of trash and manure lining the streets and sinking in to the creosote brick lined streets kept the crowds down in most parts of the city. Much of the industry had collapsed, some joked the only industry still humming along was the mosquitoes that threatened to eat you alive of a night. The federal government had sent the military in a time or two to make sense of things, but all in all most decent folks or ones who had the means had left, leaving a host of poor immigrants and those who preyed on their fellow man for a living. It had seemed like a perfect place to disappear for a while.

A few of the glances I was getting made me think the owner of the roving eyeballs was trying to figure out just how much money I carried on my person, perhaps the fancy duds weren't the best idea. Still, I was wearing two guns, and only the truly desperate tried to rob an armed man. One feller dressed even fancier than I was came tearing out of an alley, his scalp pouring blood all over his starched yellow shirt, throwing up a ruckus about how someone had knocked him over his bean and taken his money. No one moved to help. I couldn't figure why more of the folks who obviously had the means didn't wear a gun. Maybe for the upper crust fellers it wasn't considered polite or something. I'm sure some of them had .22 and .25 caliber hideouts on their person, the general stores were full of them, but I much prefer it when folks have all their cards on the table, and everyone knows what's what. I'll allow that's a bit two faced, seein' as how I had three guns hidden and out of sight on my own person.

The whitewashed steamboats gave way to creaky fishing trawlers and ugly buckets covered in tar, unloading all manner of cargo. The crowds thinned a bit, and most of the folks around me were engaged in some kind of good honest work. I felt sorry for them.

I'd worked awful hard all my life, but hardly a bit of it was what you'd call honest. I was taking a step forward in that direction of late, I suppose gambling was a step above taking money at gunpoint from trains and banks and such. A little bit at a time.

From what I knew of these men, they'd been able to follow us at will, up and down the river, thought the water leaves no trail, and you couldn't track a man through a city like you'd track a deer. They were either very good or they had people everywhere. These men knew how to follow me through the places where men dwelt, but what about the wilderness? Out in the open country of the west they'd caught up to us, but there were only so many towns, and a man traveling in a wagon with a pine box in the back and a big dead horse covered in a tarp wasn't hard to inquire after. We'd see how they'd do with a lone man in the woods.

I hadn't wanted them to think I was onto them before, but now I wanted to disappear from their sight. If I was lucky they'd be angry about two of their men being killed on top of however many I'd gunned down last night, and they'd go a mite farther than discretion allowed. They seemed to want to kill me outright, so I was betting they'd follow.

Suddenly, I turned off the dusty lane and into a tangle of trees at the roadside. I dropped low then and moved quickly, but didn't try to cover my tracks. I wanted them to follow me in, and if I was lucky they'd be just dumb enough to do it.

These men were like as not city folk, so I didn't want to make it too hard for them. I even broke a few branches along the way, laying a straight path until I turned and doubled back on my trail. What I'd just done wouldn't fool a knee high injun, but this was a new kind of game to these men, else I might be dead in a few moments. Another gamble.

I didn't have to wait long. Two men marched into the woods, crackling like a herd of cattle stampeding through a tumbleweed party. I held my breath as they came closer, following the trail I'd left for them. For not the first time I hoped they wasn't playing dumb just like me. The brush was thick behind me though, and even if they caught on to my plans, they'd have to come through it, and there was no way to go quietly through that tangle.

Two men came into view. I was tucked well back into the overhanging branches of a willow tree; I didn't think they'd see me. All their attention was on the deep footprints I'd left in the soft ground.

They were of average height and build, dark complected, unshaven, looking for all the world like a pair of day laborers from the docks just a hundred yards away. They were good. But not good enough.

I eased out from under the willows, glancing back down the trail to make sure there weren't more of them in tow.

So far, so good. I crept up behind them on cat feet. I had both guns in my hand; this would be like a good old fashioned stick-up. Hadn't pulled one of those since my youth, long ago. I even felt a wave of nostalgia. I'd been trying to turn over a new leaf since I was a man hitched, and a little more aware of the condition of my immortal soul, what with nearly losing it and all. I had to enjoy these things while I could.

"Reach for the sky fellers, nice and easy!" I drawled in my best bandito voice.

The men froze, and lifted their hands like I'd said, nice and easy.

"Turn around, and don't try nuthin'," I warned, "Or I'll fill you so full of holes you'll look like one of them trawlers on the docks."

The men glanced at each other, and hesitated. I almost fired, I was sure they was gonna' do something foolish, but they slowly shuffled about to face me.

Their's were the eyes of fanatics, burning with passionate intensity. My hopes fell right then; they weren't likely to give up anything about where they were holed up, or how many of them there were, no matter what I did to them.

Stars burst in my head and my knees went weak. My guns fell to the ground from limp fingers, and I followed a moment later. Before the darkness washed over me, I looked up into an angelic face. It was smiling at me.

The effect was not comforting.

CHAPTER 4

A hatful of stagnant water from a nearby pool woke me from my slumber. I was bitter about the fact that they'd used my hat, and even more so about finding myself pinned down with one man kneeling on each of my arms.

"It is time to confess your sins, my son."

There was that angel face again. He squatted over me, pale white cheeks over cupid bow lips, he looked all of fifteen years old, but his pale blue eyes told a different story. They burned with a mixture of delight and madness.

I shook my head to clear it of the cobwebs, and all I got was a burst of pain. That helped wake me up some, at least. My vision still swam a bit, but I was aware enough to know I was in deep trouble. Especially since my guns was tossed in the dirt a few yards away.

"Where is the demon?" The cherub asked in a lilting voice. The notes were full of mercy and understanding.

"What demon?" My head was still awful foggy, It felt like fingers were running through my brain, searching.

"The one you call your bride, the abomination." His words made my blood boil, but at the same time were so gentle, the tone so innocent, it seemed perfectly reasonable to just tell him what he wanted to know.

"She's my gal, and she ain't no demon! She's got a soul, same as you'n me!" I resisted, though I felt like I was making a fool of myself in doing so. What was going on here? Had to clear my head.

The angelic priest frowned at me, looked thoughtful for a moment. Then his bright eyes hardened.

"She is cursed, as is all her kind. She feeds on the blood

of the innocent; her very existence on this earth is an affront to God. It is not too late for you. Your soul is rotten, but not irredeemable. Tell us where she is my child, and take the first step towards cleansing your conscience."

Those silken tones rippled through my mind. I steeled my will, though against what I didn't know. They wasn't torturing me, and I didn't guess they thought I was just up and gonna tell them where my beloved lay helpless. They was using some kind of influence on me. Was I mesmerized? I had to hold on to what I knew for sure, there was no way I'd lead them to Maria, so they could just get on with the torturing. I almost wished for it, it was preferable to having that feeling of something picking at my brain.

"No use kid, I'm at least twice your age, but more'n that I'm not saying. Maria, or Mrs. Wilder to you fellers, ain't never killed a man what's still been living. On the other hand, I've killed and robbed and stole whatever ain't been nailed down my whole life. You want to cleanse the earth of something bad? Start with me and then include yourselves after. You could do that the other way around too, and I wouldn't complain none."

"Please Father, let us kill him! We can find out what we need to know after he's dead. The Saint will understand."

Something about that comment chilled me. I didn't want to show it. Slowly, I felt those spectral fingers recede, and my thoughts were my own again.

"Silence, Brother Lawrence, is a virtue. Do your best to remember that."

The two monks kneeling on my arms nodded and shut up right quick. My arms was going numb.

"You fellers are more'n welcome to kill me now, if'n you can manage it. I don't know how you plan to get anything out of me after I'm dead though, I'm thinkin' I'll be a mite less talkative."

The little priest smiled ruefully.

"There is much you have not seen then, cowboy. Pray

it remains that way. Our order is sworn to fight evil wherever it may exist, especially against the creatures that have no business on this side of the veil. Your demoness, sweet though you may think her, will turn on you in time. You say she has a soul. Demons do not have souls, not such as we do. You say she has not yet taken a victim, but that will change. Her thirst will grow, of this I am sure. It always wins. And then that blood will be on your hands. It would be on mine too, were I to show you mercy. I will give you one last chance to save your soul before you meet your maker. Make a confession to me now, unburden your soul, and I shall take care of the rest. Would you not rather meet your maker with a clean conscience?"

I grinned.

"My conscience, such as it is, ain't likely to be cleaned. The only way I'm gettin' to paradise is if the Lord's feeling mighty free and easy with the entrance, or if ol' Pete ain't watchin' the pearly gates none too close. So if it's all the same to you, I'll just tell you to get stuffed and take my chances."

The cherub sighed and pulled a thin cruel blade from his frock. The handle was shaped like a crucifix.

He closed his eyes and raised the blade high, whispering something. A prayer perhaps, or a curse upon my soul.

At that moment, I dug in my heels and bucked my hips upwards, hard. I was just funnin' about them bein' welcome to kill me and all, I didn't plan to go out so easy.

The child-priest fell forward, his blade stabbing into the throat of the man on my left arm. That was helpful. The monk what got stabbed rolled away gurgling and spraying blood, and I felt the feeling shoot back into my arm, all pins and needles. I couldn't do much else with it yet, so I balled up a fist and let the kid have it right in those fat, pouty lips of his.

He spun off me and hit face first into a tree trunk. That was just a bonus. The second monk dove for my guns, but I caught hold of his boot and he fell just an inch short. With all the power of my arms, I dragged myself over him clutching handfuls of trouser and jacket and hair until I grabbed hold of one of the Colts. His hands were scrabbling for it too, but I kept a tight grip on the barrel and snatched it back over his head. He didn't have the leverage to hold on, so he let go and went for another gun. Just as his fingers closed on one, I brought the Colt down hard like a hammer on the back of his head. He went limp and collapsed to the ground.

I used my boot to sweep the guns away from his hand, searching around for the little priest. He was gone; the only trace of his was a trickle of blood where his pretty little face had lost a butting match with the tree trunk.

One man dead, one man gone, the other unconscious. You play the hand you're dealt.

Keeping wary in case the priest returned with more monks, I fetched up my shooting irons and melted back into the trees. I'd cleaned up the crucifix dagger and turned it over and over in my hands while I waited. The handle was made of gold, but the blade appeared to have a silver inlay in a sort of ribbon pattern all the way down to the tip. It would have been a handsome blade if I ignored the fact that it was very nearly buried in my chest. That little detail kind of soured me on the whole affair.

I'd hit the monk pretty hard, but he must have been sturdy, because he was up and on his feet in only a few minutes. It was awful chancy, given that they'd turned the tables on me so easy before, but I might not get another chance to find out where these coyotes were bedding down at night.

I kept away back for the first half an hour, which was fine since the monk wasn't too steady on his feet, and I kept him in sight easily. I stayed too far back for him to make me out, but that red plaid shirt he was wearing stuck out like a sore thumb in the growing crowd. He made a beeline for the other end of town. I guess he wasn't thinkin' someone might follow him for a change.

Once in a while he stopped and leaned against a post. Must've still been pretty dizzy. I took my time and didn't rush things; I couldn't afford to spoil this now. It was over two hours before we made our way to the other end of Memphis. Again in the outskirts, the crowds were less and I had to fall back a ways to keep from being spotted. From time to time I checked my own backtrail, but no one stood out and I didn't notice the same faces more than once.

My quarry turned down a long, lonely road, and for a moment I feared he might be leading me into a trap the same way I had done before, but I wasn't turning back now.

There was no one else on that road, so I stepped off to the side and followed from the thick trees and bushes. Keeping an eye on the monk and just about everywhere else was tricky, but my head still ached from the bushwhacking I got and I didn't aim to repeat the experience. Unless it involved smacking that kid around again. That might be worth it.

The monk paused and looked around for a minute outside of an old stone church at the roadside. Some of the stained glass windows were broken, and the roof had sunk in here and there. I stayed as far back in the greenery as I could while the monk assured himself he was alone.

Then he went inside.

I smiled to myself. Gotcha.

CHAPTER 5

One gun drawn, I crept out of the woods and up to the door of the church. No sounds echoed from within the darkened door. I guess it should have been fittin', even obvious that a group of assassin-priests would choose an abandoned church for their hideout. Then again, looking back, a man always sees clearly.

I took a deep breath and plunged in, thinking along the way it might be wise to have some sort of a plan. In that same moment, my plan was crystal clear. Shoot everything that moves.

It wasn't such a great plan, since all I saw were a few splintered pews and shadows. A few spots where the roof had caved let in bright beams of light. I managed to avoid the piles of rubbish and debris on my way to the altar. I was pretty sure I could hear a whispering coming from somewhere. The barrel of the Smith led the way as I searched high and low, but I couldn't find the source of the voices.

All of a sudden, I got dizzy and felt weak in the knees. My vision started to go dark. Not now! I guess taking that big knock over the head was having some after effects, but I could ill afford them. My stomach wrenched, and in the next moment I spewed bile over the stone floor of the church.

The whispering stopped instantly. I heard footsteps echoing from somewhere below me, and the grating of stone on stone. The floor at the foot of the altar began to shake, then move. I took a few stumbling steps and threw myself across it. The stone shoved against me, but I'm a bit on the stout side, and the door or whatever it was didn't open, though someone was shoving against it hard. Another pair or two of hands must have joined in the effort, because the stone bucked up hard and nearly threw me off. The second time they shoved it, I jammed the barrel down in the crack and pulled the trigger. A shout and then there was silence, they must have decided it wasn't a good time to try and force their way through. It wouldn't last long; I had no idea how many of them were down there, or what weapons they had with them.

The wood and stone altar was big and sturdy, but so was I. My bout of weakness and nausea had passed, and I grabbed hold of that slab of stone and pulled with all my might. I had to hitch and yank, but that stone began to move, and I kept pulling till the bulk of it rested squarely on the false stone trapdoor.

Any smart fox knows to have a bolthole in his den, and these fellas were sharp and canny enough to have one as well. They'd be coming out in mere moments, armed to the teeth, and I needed to find where they'd appear. I knew if I wanted an escape route, I'd put it outside the church, well into the woods. That was where I needed to be.

I ran out of the church and into the woods, guided by a feeling more so than reason. Swinging around the building once I was in the trees, I ended up right behind the tall stone structure. A section of the ground nearly exploded upwards, and men in black frocked coats burst into the light.

My guns bucked as I slowed to a walk, bringing the Smiths up one after another. One man went down with three slugs in him, the next took two, and I winged a third. Dropping the Smiths, I fetched out the Colts and continued to deliver .44 caliber justice to Maria's tormentors.

The peacemakers finished the job on the one I'd winged, and then another man came out, raising a Winchester. He was too slow by a sight, these priests were better with blades than bullets, and I dropped him before he could so much as draw a bead, putting a pair of holes right above his heart.

They stopped coming out of the hole then, and all was

quiet as I stood just off to the side, so anyone coming out would have to turn to face me, and in a different spot from where I'd fired last.

I had them pretty well covered, or so I thought. Until the bundle of dynamite flew up out of the hole, the fuse crackling and smoking down fast.

I almost turned and ran, but another idea struck me right after that thought. With every ounce of speed I could muster, I ran up to the dynamite and booted it hard, right back down into the hole. There was a second's worth of panicked shouts, and then I threw myself to the ground and pulled my hat down over my ears, just in time to get punched in the gut by the earth itself, the blast shooting black smoke and shrapnel out of the hole in the ground only feet away.

Coughing from the sulfurous air, I dragged myself to my feet and stumbled out of the cloud of smoke still belching from the tunnel below. My ears were ringing with a high-pitched whine.

Moments later, I was hard at work shoving the stone altar off the trapdoor inside the church. Tendrils of smoke rose like searching tentacles from the hole below. It was a good bet no one had survived. When the haze cleared, I cautiously climbed down the ladder, one hand filled with a Smith and Wesson.

I dropped into a crouch at the foot of the ladder and waited, my ears straining for any sound of life. I didn't hear none, but with my ears ringing like they was I wasn't like to hear much. I slinked along as close to the wall as I could, mindful that this old church might have been none too sturdy before fellers started settin' off dynamite underneath it.

It was pitch black down there, just a trace of light at the other end of what I got the sense was a large room, square built directly underneath the church. I edged forward in the darkness until my eyes adjusted. I still couldn't see much, but a few boxy shapes in the middle of the room caught my eye.

Crouching low, I struck a match well away from my vital parts, but no gunshots rang out of the shadows. The floor was littered with shredded cots, chairs reduced to kindling, and a stack of boxes with the lids busted off them and some of the planking too. I stuck my hand in one of the boxes and came up with a familiar feel. Bullets. Lots of them. Holding one up to the light, you could see .44-40 marked clearly on 'em, and the slug itself was bright and shiny. Silver. I tried to remember what I'd heard about silver bullets before. Miguel Cortez had spoken to me about how they was useful for some things, that his order had a host of tools to use in their battle against evil creatures. I guess I would have paid more attention if I wasn't so focused on the vampires trying to eat me and Maria alive at the time. Something about how silver would hurt worse for a vampire, but wouldn't kill it outright.

If I hadn't wiped out the whole gang right here, I had a hunch they'd be along shortly, so I just stuffed my pockets full of the bullets. If nothing else, it was an awful stylish way to shoot a feller, and all that silver would be worth more'n a few dollars. The way I looked at it the order of Saint Michael was just reimbursin' me for all the bullets I'd been handin' out left and right to their folks.

There was more down there too, bits of paper with writing on it in some other language, some Latin, and something else entirely. There was an assortment of once handsome blades strewn about by the blast, now bent and blackened. I fetched up one interesting looking tome, the leather was covered in soot and ash, the ends of the pages still smoking. Brushing off the embers, I opened it where a ribbon had marked a particular passage and struck another match.

There was Latin on one side, and what looked like English on the other. I say looked like because the spelling was even worse than mine. It took some puzzling out, but what I read was mighty interestin':

THE CHOOSiNG IS THE DAMNATION OF

THEYR SOUELES. WHEN A MAN A VAMYRE BECO-
METH, HE BEWRAYETH ALL GOD'S MERCY, AND
WILLFULY EMBRACETH DARKENESS. BUT IF IT BE
THAT A MAN DOTH NOT MAYKE HIS CHOYCE, AND
BECOMETH A VAMPYRE BY OTHRE HAPPENYNGS,
HE SHALL BE WOT TO KEEP THAT SOUEL, LEEST-
WAYS TIL THE TYME WHEN HE HYMSELF SHALL
CHOOSE TO DYVEST IT LIKE A SNAYKE DOES ITS
SKYN.

FOR THE DARKENESS CALLS TO HYM, AND
THOUGH HE RESYSTETH, IT IS NOUGHT BUT A
MATTER OF TYME TIL THE CALL WAXETH TOO
STRONG TO RESYST. AND THAT MAN SHALL FYN-
DETH HYMSELF AS DAMNED AS HE WHAT MADE
THE CHOOSING. FOR THE SPILLING OF INNOCENT
BLOODS IS A SYN AS DAMNING AS CAIN'S OWN.

A sudden rumble above me told me it was time to abs-
quatulate this particular address, and the caving in of the
tunnel a second later just confirmed my hunch. The match
burned down to my fingers at that moment, and I pulled
back, dropping the little stick of flame right on the page I
was reading. The whole book went up like a funeral pyre.

I dropped it and started stamping, but those dry pages
lit up like so much tinder, and the book shredded under my
boot, burning sheets of parchment floating up to the sky. A
stone broke loose from the ceiling above and fell near to my
boots, so I left off and ran for the trapdoor. More stones fell
behind me, and I vaulted up the ladder like a polecat, just in
time to see the floor falling out in the church, broken pews
sinking into the darkness below.

A gaping cavern was opening up where the floor used
to be, I was trapped at the back of the church. A few of the
rafters broke loose of the remaining roof and swung wildy
before dropping into the abyss. Frantically, I searched for a
way out.

A busted up stained glass window stood high to my right,

letting in the light where panes had fallen out, and coloring it red and blue and yellow where it hadn't. Wrought steel provided the frame itself, and there was no way I was busting through that.

The crossbeam that held the rafters broke free at one end, smashing to the stone floor almost at my feet. One end was still attached, leading upwards towards the other end of the church. I didn't have much choice.

I leapt onto the broad beam and ran up it like a squirrel, only slower and less graceful, which is to say like a man scared out of his wits more than a squirrel, I reckon.

The beam shuddered as stone and wood fell and crumbled and caved, and I was near thrown clear more'n once. By sheer force of fear and desperation I clung to the beam, staying low and using my arms for purchase where I could find it, for balance where I could not. I was near the end, all I had to do was get a few more feet and jump down, run out the door and-

A sudden violent tremble sent the beam a'shivering, and I lost my footing and slipped off to one side. My hand caught hold of an old knot in the beam, but there was nowhere to dig my fingers in, and my other hands vainly sought purchase on the smooth dry wood.

I happened to glance to the right, towards the back of the church, just as the stone supporting the fallen beam gave way. The log rolled, shifted, and both of us plunged down into the rubble. I looked up as I fell, the remaining rafters were following me down.

CHAPTER 6

I thrust one arm up atop a hunk of stone, and pulled myself up another foot. By chance or some other force, I'd fallen right into a pocket in the rubble, only able to curl up in a ball and hope against hope while stone and wood fell all around me. After a while, it had stopped, and I'd been busy picking my way up out of the wreckage for the better part of an hour. I was covered in lumps and bruises, but somehow nothing felt broken, and my new duds was ruined besides.

I threw the other arm up, and pulled myself up into the sunlight. Only the back wall of the church stood, the crucifix still hanging larger than life above where the altar used to be.

"Don't know if you had a part in this," I drawled, "But if'n you did, I'm much obliged. Sorry about your house."

I pushed myself up to my feet and staggered out of the ruins.

I paused there for a minute, my hands on my thighs, just trying to breathe. I felt awful dizzy again. I didn't dare hang around, so I pulled myself together and hobbled off down the road. The toe of my boot was split open, and the heel had been knocked clean off the other one. My jacket was ripped at the shoulder, and one pocket hung halfway off. My trousers were ripped at the knee and up one leg. At least my hat was fine and dandy, needing only to be smacked against my thigh a few times to knock the dust off. Small favors and such. I was awful fond of that hat.

It took me twice as long to get back to town, and the sun would be going down soon. The thought of seeing Maria shortly brought a smile to my cracked lips. The day hadn't gone quite to plan, but I'd struck a definite blow against our enemies, and that felt good after so long on the run.

I'd spent most of my life on the dodge; it was just a matter of my career, such as it was. A choice. It felt different not being able to stop running. Out west it was just a matter of swapping out a name, and moving to greener pastures, where if you weren't known, nobody cared to ask about your past. This was different. There would be no reasoning with these hombres. No respite. Not until they was dead and gone, or they'd done the same for me and my bride. I guess the preacher man really means it when he says "for better or for worse".

My duds were definitely for worse. As I neared the hotel where I bedded down during the day when I had a few short hours, I passed a man wrapped up in an old wool cavalry blanket, nursing a half empty bottle of what looked to be corn whiskey.

"Fallen on hard times stranger?" The vagrant asked, grinning at me through broken and yellowed teeth.

"You got that about half right friend," I allowed, and took a seat to rest my aching feet. It had been a hell of a day to break in some new boots. And now I'd need another pair altogether. I lifted up the boot what had torn open at the toe to inspect it, and the other heel fell off. So much for men's finery.

The old reprobate passed me the liquor, and I wasn't too proud to take a swallow. Liquid fire burned its way down my throat, but felt good and warm in my gut. All a sudden I was hungry again, but it would have to wait. Maria would need to eat too.

"What's your story friend?" I asked as if to pass the time.

"Name's Jeremiah Beaufort. Fought in the War of Northern Aggression, I done learned it best out here not to say which side, too many darned Yanks paradin' about for my taste," He lifted his stump of a leg, "Lost this at Antietam."

The old rebel, who'd just told me quite clearly what side he was on, held out a stump of a leg cut just below the knee, a hefty piece of wood strapped to the remains of the limb.

"Got me a medal for it, though I traded it some years back for some of what you're holding right there. Stars man! No need to drink it all, give us a pull. Glug! Now then, I didn't amount to a whole lot before the war, and nary a hill o' beans after. I split some wood when I can, sweep some saloons out on the regular, but it's just enough for a plate of beans here and there and a whole lot of bad whiskey. T'ain't been nothin' but hard times, and never will be nothin', savin' the day when that chariot swings low and takes me up, high into the sky. Till then the mutts around here are my friends, and that and a good bottle, or a bad one, is all a man needs while he's waitin'."

He drifted off somewhere, looking off into the distance, his brow furrowed, but I wouldn't have been surprised if wherever he was were the sounds of cannons and dying horses, and men screaming in pain.

"Tell you what mister," I began, hoping he wouldn't ask too many questions, "I've got a job for you, if'n you're interested. It might sound a bit strange, but-"

"Sonny," he laughed, "there's not much you could say that would sound strange. A man lives out in the street, and spends half the night with his eyes peeled, he sees some things along the Mississippi, things you wouldn't believe if I told you. Things that if a man told about, a body'd think he was plum crazy, or drunk, or both."

He could try me, but this wasn't a contest.

"Well then old soldier, I'll just level with you. I need your blood. Not all of course, just a good draft."

The old rebel regarded me sharply.

"Not the strangest thing I've heard, there've been some queer folks about that've asked me for odder work in the past, and there's some things ain't worth doin' just so's you can go to sleep with a full belly. Sure. Why not. You got money?"

I grinned, and dug a wad of dollars and few gold pieces

out of my belly band. I stuffed it in his hand. He bit down on one of the gold pieces, testing it.

"That oughta be enough for a bath and a shave, which you should consider as a public service fella', and a few crates of beans and whiskey."

"I'll be right back, if you'll wait, and if you're still here, I'll throw in a bonus."

"Mister I'm alot of things, but i ain't never took money I didn't earn. I don't know what you need my blood fer, and I don't wanna' know. But we struck a deal, and I'll keep my word. I'll be here when you get back."

Jeremiah spit on his palm and held it out, and with some trepidation, I took it and shook it.

I stalked off as fast as I could walk on my flat heeled boots and climbed the stairs to my room, aching every step of the way. The look on the clerk's face was priceless.

As I turned the key and opened the door, my hand flew to my gun. The room looked like a twister had touched down in it and decided to stay a while. The dresser drawers was open, half of 'em pulled all the way out, lying on the floor. The contents were strewn all over the room. The bed was turned over, the mattress cut open in several places. There was no question in my mind who'd done it. They wouldn't have found much. But the transfusion kit I'd bought from a doctor in Natchez was lying broken in one corner of the room. Blast it all.

I was just fixin' to go downstairs and knock the clerk around a mite for apparently not noticing a gang of wildcats bein' left untethered in my room when I heard a chilly voice behind me.

"Mr. Wilder, it's best if we go now."

I spun on my heel, jamming the barrel of the Smith into a tweed clad set of ribs. The man looked harmless enough, a prim fellow with bloodless lips and a wan smile.

"Who's suggestin'?" I wanted to know.

"My name is unimportant. I have the honor of serving

Mr. Francis Icarus, lately of New Orleans, and he bid me seek you out."

"What do you want with me fella?" I didn't know no one named Icarus, and I thought I could be forgiven for being a mite suspicious of strangers. "Unimportant" would get a bullet at the first sign of treachery.

"I'm perfectly happy to answer all of your questions, Mr. Wilder, but if you don't come with me now, we'll have to have this conversation in the hereafter. You see, the gentle-men who disheveled your room also left behind a bomb, a rather sophisticated one, which you activated the moment you opened the door."

I looked up and down atwixt the mess, but didn't see hide nor hair of any bomb.

"Oh, you needn't bother, it's quite well hidden," The stranger purred, his sharp features calm as a man out for a Sunday stroll as he produced a pocket watch with a flourish. "It appears we only have ten seconds left until it detonates, so perhaps you'd be amenable to moving along?"

I was amenable.

Sometimes it's wise to take things at face value, and so I vaulted past the stranger and down the steps in two or three bounds, and then was out in the street. He came strolling out right after, though I hadn't noticed him running.

"So where's the blast?" I asked when we were outside. In response, "unimportant" put his fingers in his ears.

The booming crack rang out half a second later, banging my eardrums about for the second time that day, and then the whole structure collapsed like a house of cards, forming a neat pile of splintered wood where the hotel used to be. I may never enter another building again, and the world would be the better for it.

"Just what the hell is going on here!" I shouted over the ringing in my ears. It wasn't so bad as the first time today, maybe my ears was getting used to it.

"All in good time, Mr. Wilder. My real purpose here is

to invite you to a card game. You've become recognized as a quite exceptional, eh, card player, and you've acquired a princely sum along the way. My employer, Mr. Icarus, requests the pleasure of your presence at the greatest gambling event ever held on the Mississippi, leaving from the dock here in lovely Memphis in three days time. You'll find the details in the card. Please don't forget to RSVP. Good day Mr. Wilder."

He turned to go. What was an arress-veepee?

"Just hold on a minute!" I shouted after him. Wincing, he turned about. I reckon I was still shouting.

"What in the Sam Heck you know about the bomb in my room? How did you know when it was gonna go off?"

He'd saved my life, but something crawling in my gut was elbowing me in the ribs, urging me to shoot him dead right there.

"I didn't know, not until I arrived. I'm only here to invite you to a card game, Mr. Wilder. I know nothing of your personal affairs. Saving your life was just a happy benefit of coincidence. If you will excuse me."

The man turned on his heel and left. I stared after him, my trigger finger itching. I supposed I was just on the prod of late, bein' hunted by Vatican assassins tend to have that effect on a man.

Jeremiah Beaufort was still waitin' where I'd left him.

"Didn't think I'd be here didjuh?" He chuckled.

"I didn't doubt it for a minute," I lied, and took a seat next to him.

"Did you bring something to put the blood in?"

"My kit got broke. You know where I can find a doctor nearby?" I asked. I would need to buy another kit.

"What fer?! Don't need no sawbones," he snorted, "When I took a bullet to my leg, it healed up just fine, without any tending to by them hacksaw artists!"

My brow wrinkled.

"How'd you come to lose your leg then?"

I took a bullet in my leg, like you might'a guessed, and lay there for a few days in the tent with the rest of the wounded, couldn't put no weight on it. It festered some, stank worse, and the sawbones said he needed to take it. I told him there wasn't no way in hell he was cutting off no parts of me, and I'd shoot him dead if'n he tried. A man can get right sentimental about his limbs. Still had my army issue revolver with me too, and he decided he didn't like the looks of that horse pistol. He left, and for the rest of the day I snoozed, thinkin' it was all over. Then a few of the men what fought beside me, only friends I thought I ever had, came by to cheer me up. Brought a bottle of booze they'd looted from a farm house when the folks living there'd run off. We celebrated; I was in such good spirits from having someone visit me I didn't take no notice of the fact that as I drank more, they drank less. Or maybe I just thought they was humoring me, being wounded and all. It's hard to remember now.

I woke up the next morning, feeling a darn sight worse. And not just from the whiskey. I went to get up and go make water, grabbed my crutch, and swung down from the hammock, favoring my wounded leg. Sprawled out in the dirt a moment later, horrors, I realized my leg was gone! The wrong leg! The one with the ball in it was still there, that thrice-cussed doc must've been drinkin' himself, he put my so called friends up to it. Can you imagine, plotting against me? I'd saved old Bill from a Yankee bayonet once, and shot a man dead as he drew a bead on Clive."

"I'm sure they just thought they was tryin' to help. Gangrene can be a nasty thing."

"Nasty, hell. Didn't hurt half so bad as when your friends don't respect a man's wishes. What they did was low down and dirty. As bad as my one remaining leg was, I leaned on the crutch and hobbled my way to the doctor's tent. It was still early in the morning. I shot him dead in his own bed, and rode my horse clean out of there. I never looked back.

39

If'n they hadn't crippled me, that war might've just turned out different."

"No doubt Jeremiah, no doubt."

"Well, you didn't pay me for to hear my bellyachin', so you might as well get what you came fer. Got a match?"

I handed him one, and he struck it on the wood where he sat. He dug out an apple peeler and held the flame along the edge. Biting his lip, he sliced deep and hard along his arm, and let the blood run down. Gulping the last of the bottle, he held it under the crimson flow. It filled up awful fast, but when it did he squeezed down tight and bound a kerchief over the wound.

"I heal up good stranger, no need for to worry. My one leg recovered, but the balls still stuck in there somewhere. I only feel it when it rains. Well, whatever you needed my blood fer, hope it works out for you."

"Happy trails, old rebel."

I put the cork in the bottle as Jeremiah pulled another cork on a fresh one, and commenced to draining half of it in one go.

"Got to put back what you took out," he grinned through his broken teeth.

I tipped my hat and hobbled off.

Walking down the street with a bottle of blood isn't the most normal thing to do, unless you happen to be me of an evening, so I wrapped the whole affair up in my ruined jacket, and clomped my way into a general store that was still open. I grabbed a big canvas sack and stuffed the bottle and a few other items in it, and went to the counter.

One fresh pair of good plain western boots and a set of denim trousers and linen shirt later, I was walking towards where Maria lay still and cold as the sun inched towards the horizon.

I took extra care not to be followed on my way to greet Maria, winding my way on sore feet through town, and keeping to lonely roads on the outskirts. I passed the bone orchard where we'd been attacked the night before, and after a moment's hesitation, went inside. No one was there, so I hunkered down behind the angel statue and waited, just in case someone was following me, they'd have to come in after me to see where I'd leave. They could attack now and just get me if they'd brought enough men, and were willing to lose a lot of them in the process. They'd almost had me last night until my bride had whisked me away to safety. The thought still got my hackles up.

The sun disappeared behind the trees beyond the river, and I melted into the willows, changing direction several times so no one could head me off. The failing light from across the river allowed me to keep my bearings, but it was like a maze in the woods. All the better to keep a body from following me to Maria's resting place.

I reached the spot and set back in the woods away from where my bride and my horse would rise from the grave, as they did night after night. I built a smoke and wondered not for the first time if she dreamed as she lay in the cold ground. I'd offered her a blanket in the past but Maria'd just laughed at me. She said she didn't ever feel cold anymore, and even if she did, she had no heat to preserve. I was awful tired at the time and so I'd offered to build her a fire atop where she'd lay, to warm the earth. She didn't laugh then, but in a very uncomplimentary discourse in Spanish, told me in no uncertain terms to never try such a foolish thing. Maria, and all vampires, didn't take to well to fire. Or rather, they took quite well to fire, depending on how you look at it. Either way, Maria and flames don't mix.

It was sometime after full dark that I stubbed out my fifth cigarette and started rolling another. It wasn't good. Maria had been taking longer and longer to rise, a sign that the small rations of blood I'd been able to procure for her just weren't enough. A sudden shower of dirt spattered my face.

As I wiped it out of my eyes and spat out what I'd caught in my mouth, Maria landed and shook herself clean. Her eyes were a little wild as she approached me smiling. She didn't look welcoming so much as she looked...thirsty.

"Please tell me you brought me something to eat!" Maria glided to me, her stomach audibly growling. I know she loved me well enough to give her life, and her very soul for mine, but something about her eyes told me it wasn't wise to keep her waiting.

"Here," I offered, producing the whiskey bottle full of blood.

"You are the best husband a girl could have! I'm famished!"

Maria snatched the bottle from my hand with vampire speed and upended it. She pulled it away a moment later and made a face, her little mouth twisting up in disgust.

"Oh Clay, it's gone cold! Ew, it tastes awful, who did you get this from?"

"You don't want to know, trust me gal. I could heat it up for you if you like, over a fire."

"Ugh, no. You tried that in El Paso, remember? It gets all slimy, like drinking pudding. Yuck."

Maria steeled herself and swallowed the rest, grimacing all the while. Then she flung the bottle out into the sky somewhere. It disappeared, for all I know it landed on the moon.

"Whoa. Whoever you got that from must have been drinking since he got up this morning. It really has a kick to it."

I handed her a package, which she took with a grin. Maria never asked me for anything, but she loved getting surprises. She made short work of the paper and twine, and held the dress up to the moonlight. It was a sun dress, which I suppose wasn't fitting, but it was pale yellow and covered with flowers, and it was all the general store had.

"Tell me dear," She said, stretching out over a tree stump, apparently feeling the effects of the second hand corn whiskey. "How was your day?"

"You don't want to know about that either."

"Clay, are you wearing new clothes?"

"Yup," I grinned, hoping she would stop asking questions, "Thought it was time for some new duds, what do you think?"

Maria squinched up her nose and frowned.

"I think you still look like a cowpoke who lost his way. You've been gambling and winning Clay, why not dress like it?"

"My clothes are just fine gal, comfortable. You embarrassed or something?" I was getting irritated with her harping on my clothes. Put a ring on a gal's finger and next thing you know she wants to dress you up like a doll or some such thing.

"Wait, you never get new clothes unless you rip the old ones in a fistfight or when you get covered in blood."

I didn't like her line of reasoning. I'd promised to stay in safety today. She'd figure out pretty soon I hadn't been so good about keeping my word on that.

"You know what?" I threw my hands in the air, "Fine, I'll go buy some fancy new duds, alright? Whenever they rebuild the gentlemen's finery store, I'll go buy some more finery! You win Maria. There, you happy now gal?"

"Rebuild the gentlemen's store? More finery? Clay, what have you been up to today?"

I sighed. Though I reckon I shouldn't be proud of it, I could lie with the best of them, but somehow, with Maria, my tongue got all twisted up, and I couldn't fib worth a possum's tail.

"You went after them didn't you!"

She started prodding me all over, seeking out my wounds.

"Clay you're covered with bruises! Tell me, what did you do?!"

Maria backed up a step, crossing her arms and fixing me in her steely gaze. I threw up my hands in surrender.

I didn't feel like a staring contest, and since Maria didn't actually need to blink anymore my chances of winning were slimmer'n an Arizona sidewinder. I built another smoke and explained what I'd done that day, getting followed, the cherub priest with the mind-fingers, following the snakes back to their nest and what I'd seen in the basement. I didn't say anything about what I'd read in the book, no point worryin' her until I'd come up with a solution. I told her how the church caved in, my hotel had crumbled to the ground, about the strange man who'd warned me of danger and invited me to cards. I tried to make it sound like I was safer'n a bearded lady's virtue the whole time. I don't think it worked.

"You stupid, stupid man!" Maria cried, burying her face in my chest.

"But darlin'-"

"You told me you wouldn't go after them today!"

"But darlin' I-"

You almost got yourself killed!"

"But darlin', I just-"

"You killed men today, putting your life on the line for me, while I wasn't there to help you!"

"But darlin' I just tried-"

Maria lifted her head, glared up at me.

"You put yourself at risk Clay, just to kill my, our enemies. You should have let me help you! If something were to happen to you, you could have been helpless, you could have been taken, you could have been killed, for me Clay, you would have been killed for me! Did you ever think about how that would make me feel?"

"Well not really, but darlin'-"

"Estupido! You brash, foolish, arrogant, reckless, foolish, impetuous man!"

Foolish. She must have liked that word, since she used it twice.

"But-"

"And I love you for it!"

She grabbed my face so hard I felt like it'd just been stuck

44

in a vise, and showered me with kisses.

I might never understand the fairer sex, but I did understand that her fangs was razor sharp, and she was bein' quite reckless herself with them. With all my strength, I pulled back.

"Maria, there's more, I-"

"Quiet, brave estupido, I have other plans."

Quicker than a greased lightning bolt, I was swept off my feet and into Maria's arms. The trees were a blur as she ran with me somewheres along the bank of the river. In a flash we were back in the cemetery, surrounded with stark white marble and gray headstones.

"Maria! Gal, what in the-OOMPH!"

She had unceremoniously deposited me in a patch of thick grass.

"Saddle up cowboy, it's time to finish what we started!"

Maria advanced on me, fangs showing, a predatory gleam in her eye. A Spanish gal, and a vampiress to boot. She was lookin' a mite tipsy, and I wondered just how many bottles of corn liquor Jeremiah had tossed back today. Boy, what did I get myself into?

"Now just hold on a minute!" I said, both hands raised to ward her off, like it'd have helped.

Maria took a deep breath and fumed, blew an errant strand of hair from her face.

"We're in the same place we got attacked last night, about to do the same thing we were about to do when we got attacked! You're always calling me es-tupid-o, what you think about this?"

"Clay, you wouldn't have thought it wise to come back here, and neither would the order have expected us to. That makes it the one place we are most likely to be safe in all of Memphis. That's why it's brilliant."

"Alright, I'll allow that makes a funny kind of sense, but now ain't the time for antics Maria, we've still got a lot to do."

Maria breathed out through her teeth in exasperation.

"Clay, we are married, act like it!" She practically screamed. Then she got playful.

One strap fell from her dress, sliding down her shoulder seductively.

"Oh my, how did that happen?" Maria asked in her most innocent voice. Her smile was anything but innocent.

"Maria, I said this ain't the time!"

"What's the matter Clay?" She purred, stretching back over a headstone, tracing her fingers down her neck. "Don't you desire me?"

I growled a bit in my throat.

"Maria. It's been a long day, and if today was any indication, we ain't got time for games. There's only one part of my whole body right now that ain't stiff and aching and swollen with blood."

My bride was undeterred. Her eyes lit up.

"Did you say blood?"

I started to drag myself up off the ground, ignoring both the effect her little show was having on me and the pain wracking my frame. She pounced then, and in one swift movement pinned me to the ground, straddling me like I wore a saddle wrong side up.

She knelt down and traced her tongue along my earlobe. My thoughts got all fuzzy and thick.

"All the more reason to make time where we can."

"Ahem." A slight cough from the darkness.

Maria whirled, fangs bared, hissing. I yanked out one of my barkin' irons and pointed it towards where I'd heard the sound.

Instead of someone, all I saw was the angel statue on top of the grave, but there must be someone out there, somewhere.

Maria and I untangled ourselves, stood.

"Run for it Clay! I'll hold them off!"

"Run, what?! Gal, who do you think you're talking to?"

"Just go Clay, I can catch up. You got to kill some of them, now it's my turn!"

"Oh sure, because I'm the slow one right? I'll tell you what, gal, I don't need you carryin' me to and fro like a sack of potatoes! I'm the one what's saved your hide more'n once, while you was sleepin' the day away!"

Maria spun on me, her fangs still bared.

"And I haven't saved you? Ohhh, that is so-"

"Excuse me. I can't take any more of this."

Maria and I stopped and looked up. It would seem impossible, but the statue had spoken. Cautiously, I raised the pistol.

"Please don't do that. It tickles when they shoot," the statue said, only his lips moving.

Next the statue's eyes opened, and he stared down at us. Well I'll be...

"I was planning on watching you longer, after all, not every day one comes into being such as you are," the statue said to Maria.

"I had not planned to reveal my presence, at least until events threatened to become...impure."

Maria sounded indignant.

"We are married! How dare you-"

"It is no matter. Your existence on this plane is an abomination. You are not meant to be here. Good and evil are not meant to coexist, except in apposition. You cannot remain good, your soul will eventually be corrupted by this body you inhabit. You died, child, and you do not belong here. Your union with this mortal is unnatural, contrary to all the laws of this realm. It is a kindness I will do you both, in liberating you from this form. Perhaps you are still innocent after a fashion, and you shall find paradise in the next life. But your place is no longer here."

"Just who the hell you think you are?" I barked, thumbing back the hammer. I wasn't so dumb that I didn't get the gist of what he was jawin' about. Especially after what

I read in that priestly book at the church, the things he was sayin' were the very things I feared.

The angel drew in his wings, then stretched them wide, his chin lowering so he could fix his gaze on me. For all the world he looked like he was made of marble. His voice seemed a whisper when he answered me.

"I am Michael."

CHAPTER 7

The Archangel his'self loomed over us, wings spread wide. He cut an impressive figure up there on that stone slab, but I'd heard claims of grandiosity before, and I wasn't about to believe us so important that the most powerful angel in heaven'd come down just to get us. If he was really the archangel, I didn't figure we had much chance, but there was no harm in giving it my level best shot.

Time froze thick and solid, Michael just stood there like the statue we'd thought he was. My nerves were tense as piano strings, I was ready to unleash all twelve .44 slugs just in front of my fingers and let Michael see just how much that tickled.

"Do you wish to pray before the end?" Those stone lips asked softly.

"If you're Michael the angel, and the good Lord wants to take us, I don't suppose asking him not to's gonna' change a whole hell of a lot, now is it?"

The sculpted cheeks moved ever so slightly as one corner of his mouth turned up in a wry grin.

"It is better when they pray," he whispered softly, to no one in particular.

Those great wings unfurled as he dove off the pedestal and spread wide, and the massive statue soared through the air at us with astonishing speed, as though he weighed no more'n a sparrow.

My guns barked out a hellish symphony, and Michael's wings wrapped him up, my bullets screaming off the stone.

Maria crashed into me as a ton of stone screamed through the empty air where we had been standing. I bounced headlong, skidded off a grave, then along the ground, and then I was falling. I didn't fall long. I found myself planted like a row of corn face down in a six foot fresh-dug hole in the earth. It was soft, considering.

The trip through the air had been dizzying, the sudden stop even more so, but when I heard Maria scream, I jumped out of that hole like it was on fire and ran towards the sound.

Maria dodged left and right, a blur, while the great stone statue plowed its way through headstones and smaller statues, reducing them to rubble. Maria leapt back into the air to avoid a razor swipe from a stone wing, and then Michael burst up into the air, and swept down again, powered by those huge wings of his. Maria was still in mid leap and hanging suspended in the air, with a ton of stone hurtling down on her. I shouted wordlessly and palmed my Colts, setting the air on fire with burnt powder and black smoke from .44 caliber barrels.

It was all I could do. The bullets cracked against stone, sending chips of grit and stone flaking away onto the ground, and Michael turned his head to roar in my direction. That didn't sound like it tickled.

Maria was able to twist to the side just in time to avoid being smashed between the great winged sculpture and the ground beneath. Maria flew off into the darkness, limp as a rag doll.

The sight enraged me. My guns empty, I ran at the statue like a madman. Not my brightest moment. I scooped up the shovel near the hole I'd fell in and charged. Michael turned rising, and as I brought the shovel down, he backhanded me, breaking through the wooden handle and knocking me end over end through the air. I crashed in a heap, my ribs broken. Somehow I was still conscious. Bone poked up through the front of my shirt, jagged and gleaming white. My vision darkened.

My sight came back for a moment, just long enough for me to see a gleaming white figure striding towards me in the ethereal light of the moon. I could feel my heart beating, the sound of air rushing in and out of my heaving, burning chest. I was being stabbed through with a thousand knives. I would have screamed but there was no air in my throat, only thick dark blood which rose in my mouth and trickled out the corners of my mouth.

My sight went out again, just for a moment. When it came back, Michael loomed over me, looking for all the world like the archangel, come to carry me to a fiery furnace and toss me in. I was dying either way, I wasn't afraid of anything he could do to me.

He regarded me thoughtfully.

I guess I am just a cussed critter after all, because with the last of my strength, I dug out my derringer with numb fingers and pointed it at him. He didn't flinch back, or seek to avoid the shot. Despite the spears of bone jamming around in my innards, I raised my arm, tried to focus on the bead. The gun wavered. I fired, the bullet glanced off his ribs, knocking out a chunk of stone which fell to the ground.

Michael leaned down, gently scooped up the stone, and held it to his side where the bullet had struck. The stone glowed, melted, and then cooled, leaving nary a trace of the scant damage I'd done.

He smiled at me, a gentle smile.

"You have courage at least. Were it that such would be enough..." He intoned.

A sudden crash of sound, a familiar sound, but one I could no longer place. A great steel gray mass burst into my vision. A horse, my horse, shot through the headstones at a dead run, faster than any horse living, and he wasn't. The steeldust skidded and whirled about, his hooves crumbling up the turf like a carpet, turning and lashing out with his hind hooves. The statue turned, too late, and the steeldust blasted him with the full vampiric power of his hindquarters. Michael flew through the air like a bullet, off out of sight.

I let my thoughts drift. My arm collapsed, one shot still

left in the second barrel. It seemed a shame to die that way, a bullet unfired, like a thing left undone. Maria floated before me, in her wedding dress, white and pure. Her raven hair stood out even against the night sky above, her mouth curled in a sweet smile, just for me. Maria.

I wanted that to be my last thought on this earth, the only one that mattered. Whatever would happen next was too late to change. Only Maria's face mattered, floating there before me.

Maria.

CHAPTER 8

"I'm sorry! Oh Clay I'm so sorry! I didn't think, I just saw you there lying dead, not breathing, your bones sticking out! I panicked, I'm so sorry Clay, I just didn't think it through, I did the only thing I thought would help, Clay I'm so sorry!"

My eyes opened. I felt like a can of corned beef what someone had opened with a sledgehammer.

I tried to lift my head. Bad idea. The pain shot through me like a lightning bolt, only it hurt worse. Or so I reckon.

Maria's face was still there, only it was dirty and blood was drying on the corners of her mouth. She was in a torn dress instead of her wedding dress, and her hair was wild, but she was no less beautiful a sight.

"Oh Clay, oh Clay you're alive! I mean, are you? Oh God, what have I done!"

Maria grabbed my face roughly, looked in my eyes; her fingers started poking around in my mouth.

"Glh, ghht ghu dhngh?!"

"What? What did you say my love?!"

I reached an arm up, ignoring shooting bolts of pain up through my chest, and tugged her fingers from my mouth.

"I said, Gal, what are you doing? Unhand me already!"

"Oh I'm sorry Clay, I really am, I just didn't know what to do! I panicked! I thought you were going to die!"

My most recent moments came back to me in a flood. I had thought so too. What happened? Why wasn't I dead? What was Maria so sorry about?"

I frowned, and even that hurt like the blazes.

"Maria, what did you do?"

"I didn't think Clay, I just saw you lying there, dead, and-"

"Maria!" I gasped through the pain. "What did you do to me?"

Maria toyed with a strand of her hair, brushing it back into place.

"It was just a little blood..."

"Just? Just a little blood?!!"

"Oh Clay, I'm so-"

"Sorry! Yeah, I got that part!"

I sat up quickly. Another in a long line of bad ideas. My ribs exploded in agony. I collapsed backwards, which was even worse.

Then Maria started poking and shoving me back into place.

"Here, let me make you comfortable..."

"Maria!" I gasped through clenched teeth, "You are making me anything but comfortable! Just stop gal!"

She backed off.

"Clay, it might be ok, I've been thinking, even if it happens, it wasn't something you chose, you might be just like me, and then-"

I held up a hand for her to stop. I should have spoken instead; it would've hurt less by a degree.

"Listen gal, just tell me what happened. What did you do to me?"

"I came back into the graveyard, the statue, Michael, he was gone, but El Gris, he was there, standing guard over you, poking you with his muzzle. You weren't breathing, your bones were sticking out. You were dead. I died inside too, seeing you like that. I panicked, ripped open the wound, and bit my wrist, letting the blood flow inside you. I hoped it might heal you. Then I realized what I had done, You had bled a lot, like when I was drained and turned. After tonight, I do not know if God hears my prayers, but I asked for forgiveness for my rashness, for my foolishness. Oh Clay, if I have damned your soul, then I shall greet the sun with open arms this morning, for I will truly belong in hell."

"Whoa gal, hang on a second, no need for rash talk. Just

wait."

I raised an arm, my need to know greater than my body's pointed insistence that I be still. I felt around inside my mouth, but my choppers were still dull as ever.

"I don't think I'm a vampire."

"Are you...thirsty?" Maria asked, her eyes filled with dread.

"Yes, I forced out, but before she could burst into tears again I specified, "Only for water, or a nice glass of whiskey. Or even one of them sody-pops I had down in Baton Rouge. But not blood, if that's what you're worried about."

"Oh God, thank you, oh Clay, I was so worried!" Wet tears burst forth again, blood running down her cheeks. This time, it sounded like tears of joy.

I tried to sit up again. Still hurt like the blazes, but not near so bad as last time. In fact, I was feeling pretty good.

"Darlin', help me up. I'm feeling better, much better. It must've worked."

The moon hung low in the sky. Behind us, the sky was melting dark blue instead of black. Dawn was coming.

I grabbed Maria and held her close. I kissed her dark locks, stroked her hair. She smelled like the dirt she was covered in, like fresh grass, but most of all she smelled like Maria. My Maria. My bride.

"We've got to get you to bed gal."

Maria yawned and stretched.

"What if...what if he comes back?"

I shook my head.

"Don't worry about that now. I've got a plan," I said, which wasn't strictly true, but I was sure one was rattlin' around there somewhere in my sorely abused noggin. Maria stretched and yawned.

"Besides, he could have come back at any time during the night, when I was at death's door, and you were alone, vulnerable. He was here last night, posing as a statue while we chewed up his disciples and escaped clean away. I don't think he's in much of a hurry. I've got a notion he's the way they've been able to keep track of us, but until yesterday we've only seen them at night. There's a reason for that, I'm sure of it. Either way, I don't think he's in that much of a hurry. The steeldust looked to have kicked him across the Mississippi. I have a hunch you'll be safe for the day."

Maria grew groggy as the light cast across the sky, the sun still hidden beyond the horizon.

"Where's the horse?" I asked, and Maria pursed her lips, giving her silent whistle.

"We don't have much time." Maria said, casting a wary eye on where the sun would come up.

A great stone tomb crowded the northwest corner of the boot yard, overlooking the Mississippi through the willows. Not a bad place to spend eternity, though I didn't think the current residents got out much to appreciate the view. Not a bad spot for Maria to spend her day, all things considered. I hunkered down and dug my kit out of my belly band, a set of three twisted little pieces of metal. Going to work on the padlock, I had it open in a few seconds. My old career came in handy still.

"Come on girl, let's tuck you in."

"Clay, I think you were right, it isn't wise to stay here. Surely Michael will come back here, to pick up our trail."

"Don't worry, I'll come back with a blanket and your box and move you in a few hours. Right now, you need to get out of the sun."

I was brushing the dust off the bier with my hat when Maria went limp, dead for the day.

I laid her down on an empty stone bier, the others had stone coffins atop them.

"Goodnight gal," I whispered, kissing her forehead softly.

Judging by the angles, there was no danger of light reaching my wife while she slept. I'd come back as quick as I could anyway, just as soon as I got the wagon and found a better place to bury her. I liked the idea of using tombs though, it seemed like a whole lot less digging, and Maria was a mite squeamish about the idea of worms crawling over her while she slept.

Where had that horse got his'self off to, I wondered, watching the sky get brighter and brighter. The sun would break over the trees any moment now, and if that horse didn't hurry up, I was going to have a Canadian barbecue on my hands.

The steeldust galloped up a moment later, looking awful pleased with himself, probably on account of savin' my hide, yet again. I rubbed his muzzle, avoiding the blood still dripping from it. If we got out of this and ever settled down, he was going to cost me a fortune in horseflesh.

"Come on boy, let's get you inside."

I led the way into the tomb, the horse following behind me. We was halfway into the stone shelter when I heard a loud thump. I turned in sudden panic. He'd gone down, deader'n a doornail, half-in/half-out of the tomb. The sun would break the treeline any moment, and he'd start sizzlin'.

Desperately, I grabbed hold of one leg, and pulled. He budged, ever so slightly before I lost my grip.

No time to get a rope and wind it around something, use leverage. That horse had saved my bacon, now I'd do the same for him. Somehow. I couldn't let him down now. I spit on my palms and grabbed him just above the hooves and tugged for all I was worth, digging my heels into cracks in the stone. The heels of the riding boots held up much better. I pulled, and pulled, and pulled some more, and finally got movement. Just an inch. As the steeldust started sliding, the sun broke the sky, shooting bright rays rippling on the surface of the river outside.

The smell of burning horsehair filled my nostrils, making me want to retch. I pulled all the harder, the cords in my neck bunching up like so many rattlers. I grunted and put every ounce of muscle and sinew into the effort, sheer desperation driving me on. The horse slid along faster now, the stone was slicker than the dirt outside, and more of him was on it.

His tail burst into flame just as I dragged the last of him inside. I smothered the flames with my hat. Gooey blackened hair coated the brim. It stank to high heaven. I put it on anyway. Phew! It was too bad, I'd have to soak it in tomato juice to get that stench out. There was no way I was wearing it.

Locking the gate, I watched for a while before I left the tomb, slipped into the woods, then circled around to another spot and watched some more. If anyone was watching, I didn't want them going in the tomb while I was here. The order of Saint Michael was still very much around, and I'd apparently just become acquainted with their namesake.

As I watched the sun climb up its arc in the sky, it occurred to me that I should never have had the strength to pull a full grown horse into that tomb, much less one the size of the steeldust. What's more is that a scant few hours ago, I'd been seeing parts of my innards a man ain't never supposed to meet in person. Maria's blood must've been powerful stuff, but it hadn't just healed me. I wasn't so strong as she was, true, but it was unnatural nonetheless. I checked my teeth again, just in case. Still dull. I wanted a strong cup of coffee, but black, no blood. Maybe a little sugar.

The birds chirped and sang so merrily I couldn't help but feel cheerful. Even though an overgrown statue-archangel apparently wanted me and my wife dead, along with his priestly order of assassins, I felt good. Strong. And hungry. There was a stack of flapjacks somewheres with my name on it.

CHAPTER 9

It turned out there were two stacks of flapjacks, lovingly cooked in bacon grease and swimming in butter, that the powers that be had set aside for my exclusive personal satisfaction. I was determined to keep these down, so I took my time about them while the stable boy hitched up my day horses to the wagon, and I plotted and planned a way out of the mess Maria and I found ourselves in. It had been a while and more since I'd gazed at the back of my eyelids, but I felt just cracklin' with pep and vigor.

Makin' double sure I had some extra blankets and the big canvas tarpaulin, I stowed the steeldust in of a day, I climbed into the buckboard and slapped the reins to get us goin'. My beautiful bride might be lyin' cold and dead as she waited for me, but I couldn't say when I had last felt so alive. I was so brimmin' with good feelin' and high spirits, I tipped my brand new hat to most everyone I passed. If I didn't feel so good I would have been uneasy about the change, it was just not my way to smile and carry on such. At least, it had not been for a long time.

I passed Johanson's gallery, which displayed a handsome painted sign which read:

Today only, a display of the finest classical statuery, imported from abroad.

Below it, someone had painted in another hand:

5 Dollers admishun.

Once I got this little fluff with the demon hunters and the Archangel back of the buckboard, I'd have to see if I could arrange a night viewing of the statues with Maria. She'd been wanting to see more of American life, most of what she did see was the moon and stars, other than a theatre or two there wasn't much entertainment and culture suitable for a married woman, and the moon looked much the same here as it did in Mexico, near as I could remember.

My sudden rush of good feeling left faster than it came when I felt an intrusion. I wouldn't have known what it meant if I hadn't felt it before. Like spectral fingers prying into my head, searching. I tried to block it out, turn my thoughts to stone. I saw a familiar pair of ice blue eyes staring at me from the crowd of passers-by. The little cherub-priest. I only saw them for an instant, but I'd know that pair of eyes anywhere.

The next moment he was gone, melting into the crowd like a spring snowfall. I drew up reins and leapt into the crowd, shoving folks aside. A few people started cussing at me, my wagon blocked the street, but I paid them no attention. It was just a hunch but if that priest was somehow feelin' his way around my noggin, I'd no notion of just what he could find there. Probably not a lot worth knowing, but if he peeked in on the part of my head what knew where Maria lay still and helpless in the tomb, then she was in danger.

The crowd was thick, folks comin' and goin' all over the place, most dressed up awful fancy, enjoying the sights and sounds of Memphis. I shouldered my way through them like a bull, watching the little man I pursued slipping through them with ease. He was small and quick, but I was big and mad, and soon folks caught on that there was a big feller brandishing a pair of six guns running through the press, and they parted for me like the red sea.

"Just a minute there stranger, whaddaya think you're-" Started a tall skinny man with a badge on his lapel and a mustache that hung down like willow branches, afore I ran right over him. I managed to step on his necktie in passing, running as fast as my legs would carry me after the cherub who'd just had a gander into my mind. I had to catch him now or I might not get another chance, I wouldn't be able to move Maria without the wagon, and men on horseback alone would be able to travel much faster. Even if I reached her in time, I'd be haulin' her around in the open until I found a better place to stash her, and she'd be awful vulnerable.

"Hey, that fella' just stomped on the Chief of Police Davis! After him boys!"

I looked back to see three men take up the chase. I saw at least one badge, and two of them had their pistols out, the third carried a scattergun. Just what I needed. From what little I knew of Memphis, Davis was the bull of the herd, the local government being frequently removed due to bein' a low-down, scurvy bunch of hombres. I'd never met Davis until just now, and thankfully neglected to properly introduce myself.

The little priest up ahead darted into a store, and I poured more coal on the fire and chased after him. I rushed headlong into the door he'd entered, just in time to have a bright flash of light hit me full in the face.

I was near blinded by the sudden light, and the photographer shouted as the couple dressed in their Sunday best screamed in protest. Spots of color swam before my eyes, but I found the back door and rushed through it into the alley beyond. The priest was halfway up the alley, running hard.

I was catching up. Despite knocking hard on death's door just hours ago, I was easily bearing down on my youthful quarry. He cast a panicked glance over his shoulder, eyes wide, but then he grinned, and darted off to the side.

I moved to follow, but as he turned the corner down yet another alley a shot rang out, ricocheting off a barrel right beside me. I jumped back as two more bullets kicked up dirt just past me. Taking cover behind the barrel, I fetched out a shooting iron and played a six note tune for my pursuers. The two men in the doorway of the photographers shop leapt to the side, and I moved to switch guns. The man with the scattergun suddenly filled the doorway, and I had to duck back behind the barrel. Two blasts and a sudden rushing of water later, I threw a careless shot back in their direction and raced off after the priest.

He was nowhere to be seen, so I climbed a ladder quick as a coon does a tree and looked around. I saw a flash of black two streets over, heading between two buildings. The structures in this part of town were close together, so I took a running leap onto another rooftop, and continued my pursuit that way.

Another shot rang out from behind me, smashing a roof tile. I ducked low and kept running, not wanting to get shot, but unwilling to lose the priest either. Dodging the law was perhaps my oldest hobby, but doing it while chasin' somebody else was a new trick.

I leapt off an awning and hit the ground running only paces behind the cherub. He didn't look so sly now. I wasn't by nature much of a sprinter, but I ate up the ground between us like the stacks of flapjacks I'd had earlier, and in seconds was right on top of him. I grabbed hold of his coat but he ducked and whirled, shrugging out of the garment. I tossed the frock away and ran after him.

The priest ducked into a butcher's store, bowling over a patron with a paper bag full of sausages. I vaulted over him and the sausages and followed the priest into the back. As I turned the corner all I saw was a sudden flash of steel. I ducked the butcher's knife hurled at my head and heard a scream behind me. Must've hit somebody, but at least it wasn't me.

The priest snatched a cleaver off the wall and came at me, snarling. Sides of pork and beef hung all over the room, suspended from the ceiling. I dodged the first swipe, then the second, and the cleaver sunk deep into a set of ribs that thankfully belonged to a beeve who was long past caring rather than my own. My ribs had already suffered enough abuse of late, so I grabbed hold of a great slab of meat and sent it swinging as the priest fetched up another blade.

He came at me with a boning knife, thin and cruel. I

raised my gun, but the priest ducked off and away before I could draw a bead. He crashed through the sides of meat, sending more of them swinging. The room was dimly lit, only a lantern casting wild moving shadows as the hunks of meat all started bumping into each other. The priest was in there somewhere, the door was behind me, and now I had to search him out among the maze.

A knife is just as deadly as a gun, if not more so at those close quarters, a blade'll cut a much bigger hole in a man than a .44 will. I had to be careful. I kept moving, trying to watch all around me. I figured as long as I didn't know where my enemy was, it was better to be changing positions rather than just a'settin' there waiting for him to sneak up on me.

And there it was. A little pair of boots peeked out at me from behind the swaying slabs of meat. I crept up on cat feet, then shoved aside a slab and thumbed back the hammer, ready to add a few ounces of lead to the priest's tiny frame.

The only trouble with my plan was the pair of boots was empty, just settin' there without their owner.

The attack came from the right, a slashing assault with the boning knife. I backed away, using my gun to catch one slice on the barrel, then leaping back to avoid the next. I fired too fast, pitting anotherwise good tenderloin, and then the priest was gone. Men were shouting outside the butcher shop, it wouldn't take long for the lawmen to find the source of the ruckus and I'd be trapped in the back of a butcher shop, outnumbered and outgunned. Well, it wouldn't be the first time.

Another cleaver laid on a cutting table next to me, swarming with flies. Fetching it up with my left hand, I resumed my hunt. Whatever happened, I needed to stay between the priest and the door, or he might slip out and escape without my even seeing him. I had to find him, and fast.

That's when the lantern crashed to the floor. The flaming oil spread fast, and I retreated from the flames. A door slammed shut behind me. I heard the lock turn a second later.

"You men, he's in there. The brute attacked me!"

"Father? You all right? Where's your shoes?"

"You've got to stop him, he's a madman! Careful, he's armed! I locked him in the back room!"

The little priest spun a good tale. It was a neat trick, and he'd bottled me up good. The deputies who was chasin' me had been awful quick to start shooting, and I didn't think tellin' them I didn't want this fight would help me none. The knife the priest had thrown had cut someone out there bad, they'd blame that on me too. For once I didn't really have a quarrel with the law Other than a few potshot's they'd taken at me, I didn't have much reason to kill these men. But here I was, trapped like a rat in the back room, and they would come in after me.

I was wrong about them coming in after me. As I wrapped my bandana around my face to keep out the smoke, bullets came through the door instead of men. I hunkered down low, watching them beeves get tore up something fierce. A few splinters of wood buried themselves in my cheek as the slugs chewed up the door. The flames rose higher and higher. This little party was turning into a barbecue.

The walls were thick and solid. Even though I took a few running leaps at them, they hardly shuddered. I wasn't goin' to bust my way out of there. The room filled up with smoke, choking my lungs even through the bandana. The firing dwindled.

"You in the back, throw down your guns and come out with your hands up! "

"I got no quarrel with you!" I tried.

"Like hell you don't. You assaulted the chief, shot back at us, and then attacked the butcher and this here little fella', I mean, sorry Father, you attacked this here priest! You surrender now, we'll give you a fair trial before we hang your sorry hide!"

That wasn't the best offer of terms I'd heard, but I was gonna come out regardless. I didn't doubt it would be into a hail of gunfire. As soon as I opened that door, I'd be as dead as one of them slabs of beef, all covered in bullet holes. Unless-

Swiftly I slashed up with the cleaver, catching the big slab of meat in my arms. Coughing harshly, I found a few lengths of rope and threw a loop over the beeve, tying it off so it hung strapped to my chest, covering most of my thighs as well.

"All right, I'm coming out!" I choked out the words, filling my hands with the Smiths. I didn't say nothing about throwing down my guns.

Gritting my teeth, I kicked the ruined door wide open. Smoke barreled out of the room behind me, covering me in a gray cloud. More smoke filled the air as the police cut loose with everything they had. I felt little shoves in my chest and shoulders, I didn't know if I was getting shot and just not feeling it, or if the beef was stopping the heavy slugs. I returned fire, snapping shots from the twin barking irons fill-ing my hands.

It was a blind firefight in a small hallway. I heard one yelp, and pointed my guns in that general direction and fired twice, shooting back and forth, trying to picture the hallway in my mind from before, and shooting down the middle, then along the walls. I didn't know where they was, but they was somewhere, and this seemed the best way to search them out.

I dropped the empty Smiths, and fetched out the Colts, moving forward through the smoke, still firing. I stopped when I had three bullets left in each gun, and charged out of the smoke and into the front of the butcher shop. Folks were scattering outside, only a few stayed huddled behind posts or store windows across the street to watch the carnage unfold.

One lawman lay dead on the floor, the other two fallen, but still alive. One man, shot through the chest twice, cussed through the blood in his mouth and raised his gun.

"Don't," I warned.

Heedless, he started to draw a bead on me. I fired, and he fell back, limp, a neat hole just between his nose and his lip. The last lawdog let his gun fall through his fingers, raising his one good arm in surrender.

He'd been shot through one arm, and the opposite leg. The leg was leakin' pretty bad. The priest was gone.

"Hold still now," I warned the wounded man, and knelt beside him, untying the bandanna covering my face. I wrapped it around the hole in his leg, tying it down as hard as I could. The flow lessened some. It might be enough.

"You...you're Clay Wilder!" The man exclaimed, then passed out. It's always nice to be recognized.

I went warily out into the street, but there was still no sign of the little priest who'd almost done for me.

"You might want to stop gawking and go get a doctor." I mentioned in passing to a youngster peering out from behind a trough.

He just stared at me for a moment and ran off.

Realizing I was still wearing the beef, I cut it loose and let it drop in the dust. There were least ten bullets in it, maybe more. There were none in me, which was good. Count your blessings and all that.

That priest wasn't dumb, so he'd be long gone. That meant I needed to get to Maria, and fast.

Running once again, I made my way back to where I'd left the wagon, but it was gone. Some no-good, low-down dirty four flusher had stolen the wagon I'd swiped when we got into Memphis. I guess old habits die hard.

I could grab a horse and ride to the cemetery where I'd stashed Maria, but without the wagon I'd have no chance of moving both her and the steeldust, and stealing horses was a good way to get even more unwanted attention. I didn't need further distraction, having the order on my tail was more than enough.

I jumped out into the street, right in front of a passing

wagon filled with barrels.

"Hey idgit, what in the sam heck yuh think yer doin?" Shouted an old man in homespun overalls and a straw hat, "Yuh tryin' tuh git yerself kilt?"

I tipped my hat and walked up to the buckboard.

"Howdy stranger, I'm here to make you an offer on this fine wagon you've got."

The old man sniffed, "T'ain't fer sale, youngster. Now git, I got me deliveries tuh make!"

I didn't have time to argue.

"How's three hundred dollars cash sound?"

The old codger scratched his whiskers, interest in his eyes. He was sharp enough to know that was at least twice was this rickety bucket of splinters was worth, barrels included.

"Got me some o' the best likker money can buy here, young'un, and the wagon alone would cost you five hundred."

Now I was getting robbed twice, but Maria was worth far more to me than all the money in the world.

I dug a wad of bills out of my belly band.

"Here's a thousand, and any more haggling, and you can do it with my friends Smith and Wesson. They're a harder bargain than I am," I said, tossing the old man the cash and pulling him out of the wagon.

The graybeard swallowed, but got out of the way as I got behind the flea-bitten nags and snapped the reins. The wagon creaked and rolled to life, and the old man went away grinning and chuckling to himself.

The wagon was weighed down heavy with barrels full of rotgut corn liquor, you could smell it from the buckboard, so I jumped in the back and started booting the barrels off the back.

"Hey, you can't do that!" One man shouted from a wagon behind me.

"I just did!" I shouted back.

Two men caught my eye, staring at me with pure malice. There wasn't anything odd about them other than the way they looked at me. Fanatic's eyes. They moved towards me, branching out into the street. I didn't know if they meant to try and kill me or just follow, but either way would be inconvenient to say the least.

"Hey folks, I boomed at the top of my lungs, waving my hat in the air, "Free whiskey!"

In seconds the saloons and barrooms emptied, store owners left their shops, and started swarming the streets, old ladies with parasols walked off in disgust, it was chaos. The street had become a pushing shoving mob, and the two men of the order vainly tried to push their way through, swallowed up in the crowd.

I grinned and snapped the reins again. There was still time.

CHAPTER 10

That wagon rattled and bucked fittin' to beat the band the whole way, but I made it. All in a rush, I jumped down off the buckboard and ran for the tomb. Halfway there, I turned back and ran to the wagon. I'd forgotten the blankets. Reaching the wagon again, I realized I'd really forgotten the blankets. I kept a stack of them along with a big canvas tarpaulin under the buckboard in the wagon I owned, or rather, the one I used to own. I cast my eyes vainly about for something I could use to cover Maria and the horse. There was nothing. I didn't dare go back to town and buy some sheeting, the priests could already be on their way here and likely were, I was half expecting them to be here before I was.

I threw my hat down and cussed, feeling dumber'n horse manure. I kicked the wagon hard. The axle gave way a moment later, and one corner sagged to the ground. I could have kicked it again I was so mad, but I figured I'd better quit while I was behind.

"Perhaps I could be of some assistance." The cold voice came from the willows behind me.

I spun, gun already in hand, searching for the voice that had sounded like it came from just behind me.

An impeccably dressed man walked out from behind the willows. His hair was slicked back, and he carried a stack of familiar blankets.

"Who the hell're you?" I asked in a gruff voice, thumbing back the hammer of the Smith.

"Merely a servant of Monsieur Icarus," the man said in a cultured British accent. I was growing tired of servants without names.

"And what are you doing here, Merely? Where'd you get my blankets? What the hell does this Icarus fella want with me anyhow?"

The man smiled, "Giving you blankets, from your wagon, and merely your presence at the biggest card game in the world, along with your beautiful bride, of course. I believe that answers all your questions."

I was suspicious. Smooth talking fellers always have an angle. Then again, so did I.

"You're the one what stole my wagon?"

"Not stolen, I merely recovered it. The one who stole it won't be stealing anything again. But surely you have other concerns. Your adversaries are on their way here now. It would be best if you hurried. You will find your wagon be-hind the trees. I thought it best to keep hidden, in case...well, in case you didn't make it."

"How d'you know so much of my business?" I asked, keeping the gun on him. This didn't smell right to me, no, not at all.

"I only do as Mister Icarus bids. Perhaps you can ask him, at the grand affair. Ah, yes, you haven't RSVP'ed yet. May we count on your attendance?"

"Maybe." I had an itch to find out just what this Icarus critter's game was. So far his men had helped me twice. I didn't like the smell of things, but maybe he could be of some help.

"I understand your reticence. Perhaps you will contact us when you have made your decision. Mister Icarus will be most pleased that you have survived this day, at least so far. I must say, it looked rather chancy there for a moment. If you will excuse me, Mr. Wilder, I do have to be running along."

I eased the hammer down on the Smith.

"You do that, Merely."

The stranger bent, put his hand under the wagon, and with a sudden movement, the wheel popped back up into place and all was right again. He climbed into the wagon and gently swished the reins. The wagon creaked off down the road, its driver somehow looking prim and proper and dignified while the big heap of wood jostled and groaned its way down the road and out of the cemetery.

I didn't know what to make of it, but didn't have time to ponder neither. The Englishman had said the order was coming, even now. I don't know how he knew so much about my affairs, but the little priest must have read my mind somehow. Neat trick, that. I wondered briefly how many times his mind-fingers had been prying into my head from a distance, and me none the wiser. He'd gotten away from me twice. The next time he wouldn't be so lucky, and we'd sit down and have ourselves a little chat over a fire. Literally.

Bursting into action, I found my wagon behind the willows as promised, and drew it up next to the tomb where my bride and my horse were sleeping the cold sleep of death. I fetched the sledge hammer out of the back and smashed off the lock with one hard stroke. Grabbing the blankets I rushed inside and breathed a sigh of relief to see Maria there dead, which I suppose says somethin' about how upside down things had become for us.

I wrapped my bride up in the blanket and tossed her over my shoulder. She'd always been a tiny gal, but it felt like she weighed next to nothin' in my arms right then. Perhaps she was losing weight, not drinking enough blood. I felt bad once again for what she'd had to do, trade in her mortal existence for this cursed one, all to save me. We'd saved each other's hides a score of times and more, but I still felt right bad about it. For the thousandth time I promised myself that if I ever found a way to cure her, make her human again, then I would do it, no matter what it cost me, even my life.

I laid Maria down in the wagon gently as I could. Now for the horse. This would be a little harder. Unfurling a length of rope I kept in the wagon, I tied one end around the steeldust's hooves and walked out the line to run it around a smooth marble pillar that held up a small statue. I'd never had cause to be glad a statue wasn't moving before. I kept my eye on it just in case.

With the horse all wrapped up in the tarpaulin, I was free to heave away at the rope. It took a lot of spit and backbone, but he moved. Putting my back into it, I hauled until his carcass edged bit by bit out of the tomb. Tying the rope off so it hung taut between the pillar and the horse, I climbed into the wagon and slowly backed the horses up along the rope so my dead steed was drug up and into the wagon by the stiff rope.

I dug my Winchester out of the buckboard and checked it. It was an 1873 model carbine, short and handy, but I had 11 rounds of .44 at my disposal, and I'd no doubt have need of every one very soon. Maria had an identical model she kept there as well.

I snapped the reins and the horses took off at a trot. My steeldust was heavy, but my day horses were strong. They'd never be sprinters, but no matter how fast the horses, when pulling a wagon they'd never hope to beat the slowest nag only burdened by a rider. I'd picked heavy boned draft horses for the task. Mules was most often used, or oxen. The steeldust hated mules, and I think he would have been plumb mortified to know he was bein' drug around by such disreputables during daylight. Oxen didn't do well in the heat, and we'd been fleeing all summer long, the draft horses pulled well at all hours of the day, though they was a bit more finicky about their feed. I headed the wagon down a long winding road, intending to put as much distance between us and Memphis as I could manage before the order caught up to us. Once they realized we'd fled, they'd have to spread out to cover all the roads, the ground was dry and it was hard to tell one wagon track from another in the dusty byways.

A sudden thought caused me to draw reins and leap out of the wagon. Crashing into the woods, I hauled whatever dead lumber I could find and tossed it onto the back of the wagon. I piled it high, covering the steeldust, banking lumber on the back of the wagon, and in between the horse and the buck-board where Maria lay a'slumbering, I piled logs all over her. The priests had shown they were willing to use guns, though they seemed to like blades a'plenty, and I knew they was packing silver bullets. Just what the silver would do to Maria I couldn't say, but I remembered what Miguel told me about all manner of different weapons they used on super-natural creatures.

I continued banking the logs high on the back of the wagon. It would slow us down some, but then we already weren't winning any speed races. The logs did provide me with some additional protection from gunfire from the rear. I had one more surprise for my pursuers, though I hoped I didn't have to use it, and I pulled the satchel out of where I kept it hidden and lay it very, very carefully next to me.

I had high hopes about gettin' away scot free, but they were just hopes. The staccatto pounding of a few dozen hooves reached my ears from a ways back. They would be on us in moments, at least six riders, maybe more by my reckoning.

A thought ran through my mind of just stopping the wagon and shooting from a rest, since there would be no out-running them. It was too risky. I might make the first few shots better than I could bouncin' on the buckboard, but then they'd be on us, and my backside would be exposed. I was a plenty good shot, but depending how many riders there were it would be easy to get swamped before I could pick enough of them off to break their charge. If I could just hold them off while we made what speed we could, it would give me more time to bring some firepower to bear on the problem. While the hoofbeats grew closer and closer, I lit the lantern that hung from the front of the wagon but left the cap off of it.

The riders came round the bend behind us at breakneck speed. I twisted about and snapped off a shot. The fore-most rider fell headlong, and was trampled under the tightly

packed horses running straight at us. The next rider in line
raised his long rifle and fired, the bullet striking the wood
piled high behind me. Not a bad shot from a speeding
horse. These hombres might give me some trouble. I took
him down with my next shot, his head snapped back. My
shot was high, but he fell from the saddle one foot hooked
through the stirrup, his head and arms dragging through the
dust. I shot twice more, real fast, and struck a horse by accident. I felt awful bad for the animal, but didn't have time
for regrets. The shot had the intended effect nonetheless,
the horse faltered and then his front legs went under him, his
rider flew forward to smash the ground head first. Talk about
bitin' the dust. I reckoned it was safe to count him out of the
running, at least for a few weeks.

There were still plenty more where he came from though,
and with return fire spattering the wagon, I dove down onto
my side and reached for my surprise. My face broke into
a grin as I pulled out a stick of dynamite. Stuffing the fuse
end down into the lantern, I waited for it to catch fire, then
watched it burn down while I lit another. I wanted them to
come fast and together, to take as many as possible before
they pulled back.

The fuses were near gone, so I tossed them up in the air
and snapped the reins for more speed.

I chanced a glance up over the timber, just as the dynamite blew. Three horses disappeared in a cloud of smoke,
bits of red and brown flew out of the cloud. The second stick
went off right after that, taking a few more of the horsemen
desperately tugging at their reins. The smoke obscured all
view of my pursuers then, so I just fired off a couple of shots
into that dark cloud and hoped for luck. I didn't get a good
count, but reckoned it was possible for two or three to have
survived the blasts. Them were some odds I could live with,
if they still wanted to chase after us. And I wasn't nowheres
near out of explosives.

I was beginning to think they'd had a fit of sense and

turned back when four riders came galloping round the next turn in the road. They were spread out this time, which was smart, if you count chasin' a man with a rifle and a wagon full of dynamite smart. Two shots whizzed by my ears, so I laid on my side again and lit another stick of dynamite. Without even letting it burn down, I tossed it high in the air. I didn't so much hope for the effects of the blast as I wanted them to focus on it. I popped up on the timber and snapped off four shots fast as I could manage. Another man toppled from his horse. The horsemen rode right over the dynamite like a pack of madmen, it blew a good distance behind them. I lit another, letting it burn down this time. Instead of throwing it in the air, I carefully dropped it just in front of the buckboard. We rode right over it, and it took a second or two before the monks saw the sizzling red stick and shouted warnings.

It wasn't enough. The dynamite exploded right under another horse, blowing its rider sky high.

I was rewarded with a hail of gunfire when I popped up to take a look. I ducked back down behind the timber. Bullets spanged and whined all over the wagon, I didn't dare pop up again, but I had plenty of dynamite. Lighting two more sticks at the same time I tossed one on each side of the road. The dynamite was sweating a bit, and one of the sticks slipped from my hand on the throw and buried itself down in the timber right on top of my horse.

Without a moment to lose, I threw myself up on the timber and started digging for the burning red stick. I expected the blast to come any moment. I was getting struck by splinters from bullets hitting wood, but I paid it no mind. My fingers closed around the dynamite and I gritted my teeth, sure the explosion would come right then. I leaned up and threw for all I was worth. The stick blasted in mid air, the explosion hurling me back onto the buckboard, but upside down. I righted myself quick enough, but my horses had broke into a dead run from the panic. I'd thought they was goin' as fast as they was able, but they'd been holdin' out on me. The wagon lurched, and just as I stood up to fire, I was bucked up and onto the pile of timber once again. A bullet creased my hat, and then one struck my rifle on the stock as I raised it to my face. The impact made me drop the long gun, which clattered off the logs and fell into the road. Fetching out a Smith, I played a six note tune with it, only managing to graze one of them in the arm. I could do better than that. I did a border shift and took my time with the other Smith. Another man bent forward in the saddle of a sudden and drew up reins. I'd hit him bad.

Another shot whizzed past my ear, striking one of my horses in the back of the head. He dropped in his tracks and his traces broke and then the wagon crashed into him, one side going high as the wheels tracked over his carcass. The next thing I knew the wagon was staying up on two wheels, threatening to tip over but the logs was piling out of it, and I was scrambling for something to hold on to.

As I scrambled up the tipping wagon, my weight shifted the balance and the whole box came slamming down hard. I lost my balance and fell headlong over the side of the wagon, just barely catching hold of the side. My heels drug in the dirt as I held on for dear life, my legs split to avoid going under the rear wheel. If'n I let go now, I was going right under that spinning disc. There were parts of me I just couldn't afford to lose, so I clung to that wood like a man possessed. A shot ricocheted off the wood near my hand. I threw my other arm up over the side, but only caught hold of a log. Another bump sent me back to skiddin' along the dirt again, barely gripping the side of the speeding wagon.

The last two riders charged, eating up the ground between us, snapping off shots as they came. One rider's pistol clicked on an empty chamber, it was at that moment that I threw the log for all I was worth. The chunk of wood bounced off the horse's head, then the rider's, and both went down in a heap. The last rider vaulted over both, and came on hard. He meant to ride me down, his last shot gone wide.

I dug for my gun. The hooves of my adversary's horse came on, pounding like approaching death. With the strength of sheer panic, I kicked both legs up in the air as the horse slammed into me, wrapped them around the thick neck, and then was torn away from the wagon. The horse panicked, having a second rider now clinging upside down to his neck, hands gripping his bridle. I didn't blame him, I ain't never rid no horse that way before neither.

A pair of strong hands started tugging at my boots, trying to dislodge me. I slipped a bit, hanging low, watching the ground fly past. I grabbed hold of the bridle again and kicked out with one foot. I hit something hard, then watched as the rider tumbled back off the horse and onto the ground. He rolled end over end behind us, until his skull hit a stone in the road in a shower of red.

The horse danced sideways, skidding and bucking and generally rebelling against my unorthodox riding style. My grip come loose and I went flying away into the bushes on the side of the road.

A few stout saplings broke my momentum, and I collapsed against the soft weeds and brush at the roadside.

My wagon had rolled to a stop some distance away, the remaining horse pulling it chomping at some dandelions on the roadside like nothin' had happened. I limped my way over, keeping a watchful eye on the road.

The wagon had a cracked axle and was riddled with bullet holes. I dug through the timber to run my hands over the cloth covering Maria and my horse, but there were no signs of damage.

I managed to creak along down the road another few miles before finding an old abandoned farmhouse to hole up in. I didn't know how many there were in the order, but I didn't think this was over for a moment. I'd killed some before, and just added to that tally considerably, but I'd no doubt they'd keep on until the evil Maria and I represented to them was put to a final end. Or until I killed every last one of them. I had a feeling I'd be at this for a while.

I didn't need anyone to tell me I was more than good with anything that threw lead, but sooner or later they'd get me, either by sheer force of numbers or the eventual turn of luck.

That wasn't even mentioning the unstoppable statue they had, the one what said he was Michael. I guess if he really was the archangel his'self, then we were pretty much done for. But I didn't intend to make it that easy, doomed or not.

Our wagon was crippled, I was plumb tuckered out from running and shootin' folks all the day long, and Maria and my horse needed shelter. The roads out here in the country was long and straight and lonely, and it wouldn't be hard for the order's reinforcements to find us. Best thing I could do was find defensible shelter and hole up 'til nightfall.

I led the horse into the abandoned barn. Setting him out to pasture out back, I looked around for a good place to stash my lovely bride. If the order caught up to us again before sundown, I wanted to make darned sure Maria was hid. They might get me, but they wouldn't find her.

I tore up some floorboards in the loft and found enough space to dump Maria in. I was real careful about replacing the boards, and then sprinkling some sawdust and dirt over the cracks. I tied the steeldust in his tarpaulin to the draft horse and together we drug him into the woods. I cut some pine boughs and tried to make the big lump of dead horse-flesh blend in about as well as you'd expect. It was the best I could do for him right now.

I took the shovel from the wagon and dug up the earth, turning it over so it looked like there was a gal and horse-sized grave out back of the barn. The ground was pretty soft, if I bought it before the night was out, they might dig a while and then some before they realized they wasn't noth-ing in the hole. That might buy Maria enough time until sundown.

All that done, I fetched the other Winchester out of the

wagon, climbed up into the loft and waited.

I didn't think I'd have to wait long.

CHAPTER 11

A spider dangled down from the rafters on a string of silk. My stomach growled suddenly, the day's exertion must have worked up quite an appetite. The gathering shadows crept towards the barn, the treetops limned gold by the setting sun. No riders came up the road, but I couldn't shake the feelin' that something bad was about to happen. Keeping one eye on the tree line behind the barn, I cleaned and reloaded my guns, one by one.

The air seemed to thicken as the last rays of sunlight disappeared behind the horizon. If the order was smart, they'd have attacked before Maria awoke. Perhaps they'd been nearly wiped out in the fight on the road. The little cherubpriest was still out there somewhere though, and as long as he was in the game it wasn't over. That much was certain. Then there was that big winged statue critter. The archangel.

He had come at us like the wrath of heaven himself. Only the unexpected arrival of my horse had saved us. I didn't think that trick would work a second time. My .44 slugs had proved little more than a distraction. Even Maria's unnatural strength had proven not enough. There was only one solution by my reckoning. I needed a bigger gun.

The attack came swiftly, just as the growing shadows stretched over the barn like a grasping hand. I slapped and scratched, but the mosquitoes were just too many. I came very near to fetching up the Winchester and throwing down with the little critters, but my hat proved just as deadly and not near so loud. I'd read in the papers of a Sunday where some educated feller was claiming the little bloodsuckers might be responsible somehow for spreading the yellow fever outbreaks that plagued Memphis for the last few years. Sounded like hogwash to me, but all the same I didn't want none of the pests tapping into my supply. Even now much of the city was deserted, near half of the folks what lived there had fled, and not many had come back.

A crashing through the brush brought me over to the side of the loft in a hurry. I looked through a crack in the wall over the sights of the Winchester, but it was only the steel-dust, tossing his head and trotting out through the trees. A sudden sharp sting in my arm drew my attention. A mosquito had alighted on my skin, his sharp beak punctured my hide. He sucked greedily away as I raised my hand nice and slow. I was fixin to splatter him good, and get a little payback.

Before I could strike, the little critter shriveled up and died right before my eyes, a wing and a leg breaking free and fluttering off as he fell dead to the floor. Somethin' about that didn't seem right.

The sun was well down now, night settled in. As I waited for Maria to rise, I was conscious of a new energy. I had grown awful tired, but now it all fell away as the moon began to rise high in the sky.

A sudden explosion of boards threw me on my backside, and Maria flew up in the air, crashing into the roof.

"Ow," Maria complained, settling back down to the shattered boards in the loft.

"Where am I? Clay?"

"Right here darlin',"' I answered, hauling myself up off the floor.

"Had to hide you under the boards. The cemetery wasn't safe. We're a few miles outside of Memphis; we had a near thing of it while you was slumberin' the day away."

"Clay you look...awful!"

"Don't even start on my clothes again-"

"No, it's your eyes! Here, look."

In a flash, Maria was down to the wagon and back up

again, with her sack of the few belongings she kept. She held out a hand mirror I'd bought her in Baton Rouge.

My reflection was faint in the glass, but then it was dark. Great dark circles hung under my eyes, my cheeks was hollow, I looked like death warmed over. Even my normally tanned skin seemed pale and drawn. Now was not the time to be coming down with something.

"Clay, do you think when I gave you some of my blood, it did someth-"

"Shhh! You hear that?"

"Yes, someone coming up the road. Two horses. The riders are whispering to each other, they sound like men. They've been approaching for a while now."

Maria's hearing was much better than mine. I hoped to get on the run before any of them showed up. These men could be scouts for the order.

"Get behind me gal, away from the window." I whispered, moving up with my Winchester.

Maria frowned.

"You don't have to protect me all the time Clay. I'm a big girl, I can take care of myself." Maria huffed, snatching up a piece of wood and crushing it in her hand.

"Gal, I've been protecting you all day, it's no time to get snippy about it. If'n you want to be useful, grab the horse and whatever you need out of the wagon. We need to run for it. I killed a passel of 'em today, but I'm sure there's more, and until we find what to do about this Michael feller, we'd best try to stay a jump ahead of these hombres."

Maria cocked an ear, listening.

"They're talking about robbing someone. They plan to shelter here at the farmhouse, they've done it before. They wait for travelers to pass, and shoot them from cover. Then they take whatever they have on them, and ride back into town. It sounds like they've been doing it for a while.

"Let's hope they pass on." These two might be low-down murderin' thieves, but I was relieved to hear it. As soon as the robbers passed we'd mount up and ride hard for another town on the river. I wanted to put as much distance as possible between the last place they'd seen us and wherever we was going.

"Clay, I'm hungry!" Maria whispered, and there was something frightening in her voice.

"Just hang on gal."

"It's not so easy..."

I cursed under my breath when the two men left the road and pointed their horses for the barn.

"I'll handle this," I whispered to Maria, kissing her on the forehead and sliding down the ladder.

I eased back against the wall and watched the riders approach. The men were whispering still, but it was beyond my ears to hear what they were saying.

As they drew near the barn I spoke.

"Don't come any closer, turn around and ride."

"Who's there?!" One of the men whispered sharply, both palmed their guns.

"Someone with a rifle pointed at your heart. I'm not lookin' for trouble. You boys just ride on."

The men stayed quiet for a second.

"This is our here barn!" The second one said.

"And you boys are welcome to it. Just as soon's I leave. Right now you'd best just keep on riding, I'm not gonna be here long a'tall."

"Step out here and let us see you." The first robber said.

"Not likely. You boys are asking for trouble. More'n you can handle." As I spoke I stepped to the side, keeping out of the moonlight. If they chanced a shot, they'd be trying for where they heard me speak.

"There's two of us, and just one of you."

"Sure about that? I've given you fair warning. You fellers don't seem to be taking notice. What happens next is on you. Ride now, or throw down."

For a moment I'd though they would turn and go, but the

thought must have rankled. Maybe they liked being the baddest fellers on this lonely stretch of road, kings of a deserted barn. Pride is a funny thing, and sometimes the folks what have the least to be proud of, guard it the most jealously.

I couldn't see much but their twin silhouettes, but I heard the click of the hammer louder'n the shot that followed it a half second later.

I was already moving left, keeping to the shadows, and cut loose with the Winchester. The robber that fired grunted as the bullet struck, and toppled into the grass.

The second man dropped his gun. He quit so fast I was kind of wondering why they'd started in the first place.

"I don't want no trouble!" he shouted, hands high.

"Then you should have rode on, stranger." I advanced out of the shadows, rifle high. I scooped up his gun and stuck it through my belt.

"Now you turn around and ride, and if you so much as look back, I'll drill you through!" I threatened.

"Ok mister, just don't shoot!"

A sudden pain wrenched through my guts, and a torrent of blood gushed from my mouth. My legs went out from under me.

I felt like to pass out, but I scrambled after my Winchester, knowing I'd be too late.

The robber swung down like a cat from his horse, and fetched up his pistol.

"Not such a hotshot now are you?" he grinned in the light of the moon, "This is for Edgar."

He cocked the hammer and drew down on me.

I braced for the shot.

A blur of motion, and then I saw Maria lift the man from the ground, her fangs buried in his neck.

"Maria, no!" I said weakly, struggling up to a knee.

The robber beat useless arms against Maria's small frame. Irritated by his struggles, Maria yanked back on his head, the neck snapped with a loud sharp crack. Maria broke away, fangs bloody.

"Clay, don't watch!"

She turned away from me, my lovely bride burying her mouth in the gaping wound. If I hadn't already vomited...

By the time I got to my feet, Maria flung the empty robber away in disgust. Her eyes closed, then turned back to me, looking utterly satisfied, like the cat what ate the canary. There was guilt there in her eyes, but also delight.

"I really needed that." Maria purred, running bloody fingers through her hair. He tongue snaked out, catching errant drops of red running down her chin.

"Maria, we had agreed-" I started, but she cut me off with a gesture.

"Never to drink from the source. I know, Clay, and since I drank from you in the caverns beneath my village, I have stuck to that promise. No innocent blood remember? Well, this man was no innocent. I can smell the bodies buried under the barn. At least a dozen of them. He was going to kill you Clay. All I did was make him useful."

"Now dear, I-"

"Don't dear me Clay, you've killed how many men? I drank from a dying man, who needed to be killed to save your life. I didn't turn into a demon did I? And I won't. I feel stronger now, much stronger. We'll need that if Michael comes back for us."

She sauntered past me, planting a bloody kiss on my cheek. I wasn't no greenhorn, squeamish at the sight of blood, but yech. I thought on that some, and Maria hadn't shied away from my kisses when I'd been long on the trail, probably smelling like a dead coyote and twice as scruffy. I guess I could do the same for her. I remembered somethin' that barefoot preacher had whispered to me after he'd finished sayin' the words.

"When you go into a marriage youngster, you go in eyes wide open. After that, a body's better off keepin' 'em half shut."

Considerin' all the troubles of our marriage, this wasn't even a drop in the bucket.

I wiped the blood off when Maria wasn't lookin' and hauled the saddle over to the steeldust. Where was he?

The dead men's horses were laid out around the side of the barn where they'd run off a ways when Maria had appeared. The steeldust was just finishing up with the second one.

"You'd better eat up, you old mule," I growled, "We've got a ride and then some ahead of us."

The steeldust whinnied and trotted over to me, full of blood and good spirits.

"Clay, I'm worried." Maria approached me as threw a leg over my horse.

"We should be. The order could show up any minute. Once we get a'movin' though, the only thing like to catch us is that great big winged hunk of stone. I've still got a few sticks of dynamite left though, we'll see how he cottons to that!"

I grinned my best grin at her, but she didn't relent.

"It's not that, it's you. You don't look right. You threw up blood, almost got yourself killed."

"Probably just something I ate, that's all."

A cricket ran across the ground in front of me, I tracked it easily. My night vision was clearer, sharper somehow. My stomach rumbled, reminding me of how empty it now was.

"Where are we going? Do you have a plan?" Maria was going cartwheels and backflips across the tilled soil. The blood must have been doing her some good. We'd worried about her actually drinking from folks, taking life for a while, but maybe she was right. As long as she only drank from those who would do us or others harm, maybe it would all be ok. Whatever demon lived in her blood would gain no strength from her nourishment, as long as she did not feed on the innocent. Maybe the book was right.

"I was thinkin' we'd ride south. We need to put some

space between us and this thing. I got some ideas, but we can flesh things out on the way."

"So we go south. I'll race you." Maria winked at me and turned into a blur, racing across the field and down the road.

She was fast, with a speed no human could match. I shook my head ruefully, and grinned in spite of myself. Normally I enjoyed our little jaunts, but I kept the steeldust well under his top speed. I wasn't altogether sure just how fast he could go. But a vampiric horse was to a regular horse what a vampire gal was to a regular gal, so after I lit a smoke and took a few puffs, I figured she had a more'n good enough head start.

"Yah mule!" I taunted the steeldust, snapping the reins. He glanced back at me and snorted.

I dug in my heels and gripped the reins for dear life as we exploded into motion. My innards threatened to climb up out of my throat as rapid hoofbeats rose into a clattering, then just a high pitched whine. My eyes were wide and wild, the trees flew by in a blur. I felt like being sick but looked up at the one thing that wasn't rushing by, the moon. My vision had gone black for a second, but I held on, and soon was able to lean forward, down out of the worst of the wind. My ears was pinned back as it was, and I kept one hand on my hat, the other tight to the saddle horn.

Maria glanced back with a smile and a wink as I rode past her. I would have gloated if'n I wasn't terrified. I'd seen her run fast before, but now, full of blood, she was near rivaling my horse's speed. She poured it on for a little more than a mile before I got the courage to snap the reins again, and we charged forward, going even faster.

I darted a taunting glance back at Maria.

"What's the matter little lady? Can't keep up?" I raised my hat in a wave and grinned at her.

"Clay! Look out!"

I barely made out her words over the sound of the rushing wind, but when she pointed up ahead, her eyes full of panic,

I couldn't help but get the warning.

I strained my eyes against the night, but saw nothing in the road ahead. Looking up to the sky, I picked out a faint patch of white, growing larger by the second, rushing at us.

Michael.

I fetched my Winchester out of the scabbard, gritted my teeth and dug in my heels. The steeldust charged dead ahead to meet the assault. Michael was coming for my bride. He was gonna get me instead.

CHAPTER 12

The steeldust churned the dirt road at a supernatural pace. The winged statue dove for us like a falcon. I cracked off shots as fast as I could with the Winchester, but if I hit Michael he gave no sign. Michael spread his wings when he was even with the road, pulling out of the dive and planting his feet in the dirt. His stone toes ground long skids in the earth, sending up a spray of dirt and rocks behind him as the steeldust lowered his head and charged.

In a collision between immortal horse and animated statue, a flesh and blood man was going to come out on the short end. The steeldust seemed to sense this, and at the last moment he bucked, sending me flying off to the side. I crashed into a dried out tangle of weeds in the ditch alongside the road as I heard a tremendous crack like a thunderclap.

I'd feel the tumble I'd taken in the morning if I lived that long, but I didn't have time at the moment, so I scrambled to my feet and raced up out of the ditch.

Statue and horse lay still on the ground. Michael sat up, and slowly rose to his full height, wings outstretched. He might have been knocked over, but he was otherwise unhurt. My horse lay still, unmoving.

My rifle gone, I filled my hands with Smith and Wesson and walked forward, snapping shots. Michael turned one eye to me, chips of stone flaking off where the bullets struck. One wing folded up and over him, but I kept walking and shooting. This particular course of action hadn't helped me much before, but it was all I had. If we couldn't outrun him, and I couldn't stop him, I was gonna' die trying.

Maria skidded to a stop right behind me.

"Go on now, gal, I'll hold him off!" Maybe I could buy her time to escape.

"Stop Clay, it's me he's here for." Maria stood her ground.

"Thats' why I'm shootin' him darlin'. Now git!"

Maria ignored me and charged, launching herself in the air. Michael dropped his wing and backhanded her like he was swatting a fly. Maria crashed back to the ground, bleeding.

"What kind of angel are you supposed to be anyway?" I asked, drawing the pistol down and placing a shot, right in his glaring eyeball. A big chunk of stone chipped away, revealing a patch of molten rock underneath. Michael groaned, a low loud pitch like a bear's, and I figured I was onto somethin'.

As he turned to search me out with his good eye I put a bullet in that one too. The archangel erupted in a flurry of motion, crying out and scrabbling at his face, the two large chunks of stone that had been his eyeballs laying at the ground next to him.

I barely moved in time to avoid being split in two by a razor stroke from a Michael's wing, and rolled along the ground as he stamped the earth with a blind kick from his marble foot. While I was down there I took one more shot at the only other place I figured might hurt him. His high pitched scream told me I guessed right. The stone angel lashed out in all directions, I kept my head down and dragged Maria away from the havoc he was wreaking on the empty air.

Maria's eyes flew open, the cut across her forehead already healing up. She was much stronger full of fresh blood, so long as we could keep it in her.

"He's blind," I whispered, "His eyes are on the ground. See if you can grab 'em. As much as I wanted to keep Maria away from the raging statue, she was far faster than I'd ever be and I knew it.

Maria smiled a wicked smile and near disappeared, moving so fast she was gone and back with the two stone chips before I scarce had a chance to blink.

"Ha!" She held them up in triumph. Michael stopped his raging and turned toward the sound. His mouth opened in a roar and he charged the spot where we were, just as Maria snatched us away from it. Michael beat the air, striking out in all directions.

Maria and I stayed stock-still, not daring to move or breathe. Michael might not be able to see, but he'd take us apart and beat us to death with our own limbs if he got hold of us. I might have blinded him, but I could scarce do much more than that.

"Maria leaned in, whispered in my ear, "You see what we can do when we work together?"

I just nodded. Women pick the worst times to have the last word. My horse was knitting himself together while Michael swiped the air, trying to search us out. Bones crackled and popped into place, his head tossed and snapped straight again, and he rose.

I started motioning to the horse, spinning my hands around and making kicking motions with my two fingers, tryin' to get him to repeat the trick he'd done the last time we'd been in trouble.

He looked at me, and from the glint in his eyes I knew he understood. He looked at the statue, slashing with his wings and clawing the air with furious blows, screaming his rage at the sky. The steeldust looked back at me, shaking his head back and forth in big sweeping motions.

"Mule" I mouthed at him soundlessly. He must have read my lips, 'cause he turned around and swished his tail up at me. The message was quite plain.

Maria and I crept over the soft ground as soundlessly as we could. Maria glided effortlessly over to the horse, I picked my way across the dirt like it was filled with rat traps. My gal was giving me an exasperated look to hurry up.

I gritted my teeth to keep from snapping a response, more than a few came to mind but words would not help my situation. I must have been distracted, because my foot came down on something dry and brittle, causing a slight crackle of twigs.

Michael stopped his search and cocked an ear in my direction. He started to creep forward, feeling his way through the dark with fingers outstretched. You could almost feel his frustration when he bumped into a post by the side of the road. I couldn't imagine what it felt like for an archangel to be taken down a few pegs.

Maria looked daggers at me, put a finger to her lips like I didn't know right well enough to keep quiet, and glided over like a ghost.

Michael inched closer and closer, and was near upon me when Maria reached my side.

I hated it, but she picked me up in her arms and glided back over to the horse, and set me down with a kiss on my forehead to soothe my pride. The night was young but I already was wishing for it to be over.

I made to throw a leg over the horse, but he stepped away. I tried again but he trotted another few paces off.

I made motions and mouthed words to the effect I was sorry, he wasn't a mule and was the bestest, fastest, handsomest horse west of the Mississippi and any other river known to man. We was east of the Mississippi at the moment, but he got the message, more or less, and let me climb on. He couldn't see me when I was behind him, so I mouthed that he was still a flea bitten mule, and I was goin' to sell him to the first glue factory we passed. A man has to find his satisfaction where he can.

Suddenly, I remembered the satchel slung across my back, and eased out the three remaining sticks of dynamite. This at least, would be some measure of satisfaction. I motioned everyone to keep still while I dug out a match. Maria glared at me and shook her head.

I ignored her pointed expressions and struck the match.

Michael lifted his head and gave up searching where I'd last been, and in a flash he was right next to me. I froze, dynamite in hand, lit match burning down. I was glad my horse didn't need to breathe.

Ever so slowly, I held the match to the fuse as the blind statue moved his head from side to side like a rattlesnake, hunting for the slightest sound. The fuse caught, and startled burning. Michael reached a hand out toward the sound, feeling his way along.

I leaned out of the saddle with my arms outstretched, a big grin on my face. And dropped the whole bundle into Michael's outstretched hand. He grabbed it like he was going to crush the life out of it, then realized whatever he had wasn't me, and held the sizzling trio of sticks up to his ear.

I snapped the reins and the steeldust ran, no more comfortable around the dynamite than me.

"Happy trails!" I tipped my hat as best I could on a galloping horse.

We were a few hundred yards away a couple of seconds later when the blast went up. You could see a cloud of dust against the moon, just over the treetops.

"Clay, stop!" Maria skidded to a halt, and I drew up rein right behind her.

"This isn't the time to stop and smell the wildflowers darlin', we need to put some miles behind us."

"Don't you want to know Clay? If he's gone? If we've won?"

I leaned over the saddle, built a smoke. Normally I had to do it by feel out on a dark road, but everything was plainly visible. The moonlight helped, but it shouldn't have been so easy to see.

"Sure I do, but I'm fresh out of explosives Maria, and if Michael ain't back up in heaven playin a harp, I don't have any way to defend you."

"Why do you always feel you have to defend me? I'm far

93

from helpless Clay. We're a team, but you keep trying to get me to run off or hide behind you at the first sign of trouble. We beat Michael, because we fought together. I know you're used to going it alone, and you just want to protect me, but Clay, believe me when I say you'll always be my knight in shining armor. You and I work better as a team. If we're always trying to save each other, we'll be too worried about the other person to fight our enemies as well as we could."

I sighed.

"You've got a point, that much I'll allow. But one, my armor was anything but shiny, the one time I wore it, and two, I can't help but worry about you. I'd rather know you're safe and sound, and I can concentrate on doin' what a feller needs to do."

Maria seethed with frustration.

"Why don't you ever listen to me? You're the strongest man I've ever met Clay, but why do you have to be so...so stupid!"

"Well, at least you're sayin' it in English now. Listen Maria, I can't help or change what I am. Even if you'll always be faster and stronger than me, I love you gal, and I'll always want to be your protector. Let's just hope we're past the hard part now. We've killed a lot of these order types in the last few days, and with Michael out of the picture, all we need to do is hunt down this one little fella' and maybe a handful more, and we'll be able to ride on."

"And then what Clay? Build a house somewhere, a little ranch? Make a life? Settle down and have kids? I'm dead Clay, I don't even know if I can have kids. One day you'll grow old and die, and then what? I wander the earth alone for all eternity? I don't know if I can handle that. I...I just..."

Maria burst into tears, long streams of blood staining her cheeks. I closed my eyes. It wasn't that I wasn't mindful of what she was sayin', I just didn't know what to do about it, and I'd rather ponder the matter somewhere far away, where

I could get us re-outfitted and ready to start goin' on the offensive against the order, one problem at a time.

I threw away my smoke and climbed down off the horse. Maria sobbed into her dress, staining it with dark blood. I put my arms around her and crushed her against me.

"It'll be just fine darlin', it's almost over now. I'll take care of these hombre's. We'll ride back to Memphis, and I'll clean 'em out, one at a time until we're free and clear. It'll be alright, I know it will."

Maria looked up at me through the blood.

"Yes Clay, it will be fine. I know it will. But will we?"

CHAPTER 13

Michael was gone. Just gone. There was a huge crater in the road, clods of dirt and rock thrown everywhere, but not so much as a chip of stone.

"Maybe he went back to heaven?" Maria ventured.

"I ain't so sure he came from there in the first place. From what I heard of a time, Michael was God's greatest warrior, he beat the tar outta' the devil his'self, and cast him down from heaven. Now, I've been accused from time to time of crowin' more'n a barnyard rooster, but I don't figure on even the pair of us whoopin' the archangel of heaven. Asides, there's a whole lot of evil in the world darlin' I figure the real Michael's got bigger fish to fry than us two. There's somethin' else goin' on here, and I aim to figure out what that is."

"Maybe we shouldn't go back after all." Maria looked crestfallen.

"No, we probably shouldn't, but I aim to anyway. We've hurt that overgrown sculpture at the least, and we've got his eyes. That gives us an advantage, small enough though it may be. We put a real hurtin' on the order, but I don't figure we wiped them out completely. From what your brother made it sound like, they've got monks and priests all over the world. If we go back on the dodge now, they'll just call in reinforcements. We've got to go on the attack. Take these fella's out while we can, else they'll never stop, and we'll never know any peace."

Maria nodded solemnly. "Then we take the fight to them." Her eyes were hard.

"That's right."

We rode back much slower than we came out. Even miles away, the smell of Memphis grew stronger and stronger. We took the side paths when we was able, some were little more than gaps in the trees, the ground choked with weeds.

I rode through a spiderweb, the silken strands covered my face and hat. Cursing under my breath, I brushed it off, but the webbing stuck to my fingers and face. Something small crawled over my chin, moving up to my lips. Before I could so much as think, my tongue snaked out and slurped the little critter up. I chewed and swallowed, the spider's legs tickled delightfully on the way down my gullet. It was delicious. What the heck was that?

I would have thrown up right there, I hated spiders. But I had just eaten one right up, and without a hint of disgust. My stomach rumbled again, I wanted another. I slapped my own face, this was clearly wrong. Perhaps the lack of sleep was catching up to me. At least no one saw.

"Clay, did you just eat a bug?" Maria regarded me with eyebrows raised.

"Nope." I answered.

Maria shook her head and walked on.

As we traveled back to town, I felt stranger and stranger. The mosquitoes clouded around me, and I couldn't help but look at them hungrily. It was almost too much to resist, but I was bound and determined not to eat one more bug. I tried to think of sizzling steaks and stacks of flapjacks and fresh made donuts, but they just weren't appetizing.

We reached the outskirts of Memphis with hours to go before sunrise. We found an abandoned stretch of houses, looked like at least a year or two since anyone had lived in them. Maria ran quick patrol through the structures; her sharp nose and ears would have quickly sought out anyone squatting in the wreckage. Probably just another spot where folks had moved on in the midst of one of the yellow fever outbreaks and no one had been in a hurry to set up house and home in the aftermath.

I dug through one of the houses looking for a good one to set up camp in while Maria dug a big hole for her and the horse. I didn't want to have to haul them around in the daylight again tryin' to find suitable shelter. There wasn't much left but some old rags and some trash. The structure was near falling down, the way houses do when folks stop living in them. I knew there were houses just as old and older still in other parts of Memphis, that hadn't been repaired or worked on in the last few years, but were standing fine and strong and handsome for all that. My own opinion was that there was something about a house that died when the folks livin' in it moved on. I'd seen stranger things this last year, so it didn't seem like much of a stretch.

"You look like you're dying!" Maria exclaimed, and I near jumped out of my skin. I hadn't heard her approach.

"I feel just dandy," I lied, but I don't think she bought it. Maria grabbed my arm and held it up. Dark veins showed through the skin, my face felt bony and drawn. Maria held up her mirror so I could take a look. I didn't look like I was dying, I looked like I was already dead. My lips had a blue cast to them, my skin was waxy and gray.

"I knew I shouldn't have given you my blood!" Maria started to sob, red droplets forming at the corner of her eyes.

"Stop," I brushed one of the bloody tears away, "If you hadn't I'd be dead already."

"Don't try and make me feel better about it Clay. I'm so sorry."

I didn't want Maria to feel bad, but somehow I was suddenly at a loss for words. I couldn't speak. I wanted to say something, but I couldn't even open my mouth.

"You should lay down, get some rest. I bet you haven't slept in days," Maria said, and before she'd finished her first sentence I found myself lying on the ground, looking up through an open patch in the roof. What on earth was happening?

"No silly, not there! Let's lay you down in a bed." Maria

shook her head, puzzled at my behavior.

I picked myself up and hurled myself into the broken down bed, a moldy-looking mattress in one corner of the room with half the slats fallen out onto the floor. The bed nearly swallowed me, and I didn't feel like laying in it, but I couldn't bring myself to get up. It was like whatever my lovely bride was telling me to do I couldn't help but obey. This could be a real bad pattern to get into. I couldn't let on what was happening, or Maria would be wearing the pants from here on out. She was strong headed enough as it was.

She sat down on the bed beside me, running her fingers through my hair.

"Oh my love," she whispered, "what have I done to you..."

Her fingers felt good, her very presence made me feel all warm inside. I loved Maria with all my heart, but this was something different. I just wanted to be near her, to do everything for her, to be everything for her. I tried to clear the cobwebs that was forming over my brain, but I just couldn't do it.

"Sleep now my love. We'll-"

I was already out.

My eyes opened slowly, the sun shining down through the roof right in my face. I felt awful.

Maria was gone. I pushed myself up from the bed, stumbled over to a dresser with a half broke mirror on the wall above it. It was hard to believe the ghoulish figure peering out at me through the dirty glass was actually me. If'n I didn't know better, I'd swear I was a corpse. This wasn't no yellow fever neither, this was something darker.

A cockroach skittered out from under a board as I stumbled away from the mirror. I snatched it up and stuffed it in my mouth before I even knew what I was doing. I stopped and looked around. There was no one to watch, so I just closed my eyes and chewed. It was the most delicious thing I'd ever tasted. What was wrong with me?

Whatever it was, I'd get no answers here in this run down shack. I checked my guns and hobbled my way into the inhabited quarters of the city. I felt tired even though I'd slept for some hours, and the sun just seemed too bright.

I tried to look on the bright side of things. At least in my current condition any lawmen of the city wouldn't be like to recognize me. I turned down Beale Street and stopped at a three story general store, the biggest I'd ever seen.

A sign read:

A. Schwab Dry Goods. "If we don't have it, you're probably better off without it!" Somehow, I figured they wouldn't have the thing I needed to cure my ailments, but maybe I was wrong.

A small Jewish man with a French accent called to me from behind the counter.

"My goodness Sir, you look like a prime candidate for our latest cure all! Here, try a sample on me."

He had a thick French accent, I could barely make out what he was goin' on about, but I took the spoonful of liquid he poured out of a fancy looking bottle and swallowed it down. I didn't go in much for snake oil but right now I was willin' to try just about anything.

"There, feel better?"

I shook my head.

"Perhaps a charm shall set you aright then. We have all manner of hoodoo accoutrements and accessories, for all kinds of ailments and curses. Anything the discriminating practitioner might require."

Rows of all manner of odd things lined the "Hoodoo" section. It looked like some kind of lucky charms to me. There was feathers and little bottles of blood and pickled lizards and all sorts of strange stuff. A year ago I might have scoffed at the very existence of such nonsense, but maybe there was somethin' here could help a fella like me.

"Ailments, huh? Got anything for a wicked case of vampirism?"

100

"Sacre Bleu! Hush now man, you can't just come in here bandying that word about! There's priests been frequenting my establishment, buying just such items used to ward off or injure all manner of undead!"

The little man leaned in and spoke quietly.

"Our motto is everything you need, unless you'd be better off without it, and friend, let me tell you, you're better off not meddling with such things. Oh dear, I can see by the look of you that you may not have much choice. This is quite serious, oh yes!"

The Frenchman bent down low and started digging behind the counter. I leaned over and whispered to him.

"Just how you know about whatever's ailin' me anyway?"

"I won't ask you your business friend, return the same courtesy, if you please! Mon Dieu, here we are, just what you need!"

"What's this?" I asked, turning the little item over and over in my hands. It was a bottle of some kind of liquid, much of it dried and stuck to the sides of the bottle.

"You're better off not knowing, at least, until after you've drunk it. Just a drop now, and it will stave off the effects of the change. It's not pleasant. No need to deny it, you've got the worst case I've ever seen of any man living. But I've never had to turn a customer in need away yet, my goal is to always have anything and everything a discriminating consumer might require. In fact, you look so pitiful I'll even give this cure to you gratis, that is to say, for free. Some of you Americans don't even know your own language, I know three!"

"I speak American real good, just so happens!" I retorted. Uppity Frenchmen, always lookin' down on folks. If Paris was so great why didn't they all just stay there talkin' through their noses and such. Funny lookin' dogs too. Still, this feller was surprisingly helpful.

"Say, what's the biggest gun you have for sale?"

The Frenchman looked about slyly.

"I think you'd better follow me upstairs."

There were three floors to the dry goods store, I'd never seen so much stuff to buy.

The second floor was a sort of museum, filled with antiques. It was here where we stopped.

"No, no," I told Schwab, "I'm looking for guns, not stuff to gander at."

"But young man, this is the only way to get to the fourth floor."

Fourth floor? I'd clearly seen from outside that there was only three floors to the shop. This Frenchman might have had some inkling of the sorts of troubles I was goin' through, but now he was layin' it on a little thick.

"Ain't no fourth floor!" I snorted. No one was pullin' the wool over Clay Wilder's eyes. Not while I was above ground and kickin'.

The Frenchman just put a finger to his lips and smiled. He turned a knob on a closet door, and motioned for me to follow. I went in to the dark room, my hands brushing the butts of my Smith's, ready for any surprise.

Schwab struck a match and lit a lamp, and stacks of books, crates and strongboxes covered with dust, items with uses I could only guess at, filled the room from one corner to another. It was huge. Didn't even look like the room should fit with as wide as I'd seen the building to be.

"This is still the second floor," I protested.

The Frenchman chuckled through his nose.

"You think so? " He cocked a thick white eyebrow, "Go have a look out the window."

I raised a few eyebrows of my own and slid between a stack of leather-bound books to the nearest window. My jaw dropped so low it'd hit the floor. Memphis stretched out below the pane, we were very high. I felt like the time I rode through the Rockies, well above the tree line.

"How-" I began.

"I call it the fourth floor only because it is, by number, the fourth. Many more could fit between it, but then, even I only need so much room."

I stood gaping at all the curious objects in the room.

"I told you, we have everything! Well, excepting perhaps a few items man has no business trifling with. But enough prattle and show. You are here for a particular item," Schwab said merrily. He crossed the room, tossing me a book from a shelf along the way.

"You may find that useful. Ah, here we are."

Schwab threw open the lid on a box after stuffing keys in not one or two, but three separate padlocks.

I followed him, and gazing down into the box, felt a grin spread wide across my face.

Some time later I was on my way up the street, a good deal poorer, two big wrapped packages under my left arm. I watched but didn't notice anyone lookin' out of place, or followin' me. I'd learned that didn't mean no one was there. I just had that feelin' that I was bein' watched again. I stopped and leaned against a railing, built a smoke and tried to ignore the horsefly buzzing around my head, though my stomach grumbled something fierce. That reminded me of the small bottle in my shirt pocket, and I took it out and gave it a look-see.

The liquid was dark. The bottle must have been old, since the inside was coated in dried matter flaking about inside the bottle. What fluid was left was oily, moving slowly as I shook it this way and that. The Frenchman had said to take one drop. Well, if one was good then two would probably be better.

I opened the cap and made a grimace. The smell nearly knocked me off my feet.

I took a deep breath, held my nose, and put the bottle to my lips.

My head swam, my eyes bugged out, the world spun. The black veins receded on my arms, becoming faint tracings of blue. I felt my face, my cheeks had smoothed out some. This stuff was doin' something, though I wondered what.

I sat down on a bench and cracked open the book Schwab had given me.

The first page had some stuff about a "Lilith, first of her kind", and it didn't seem very to the point, so I flipped some pages, and kept reading:

The Vampyre has only one thought during the night. The demon that lyveth in the bloode thyrsts for more bloode, and only finds rest whence it has drunke its fille of some poor soules lyfe. But by day, when the vampyre lyeth cold and still in deathes embrace, the human soul attached to the vampyres body and under its dominion goes with it down to the fiery pit, to burn and suffer torment in Hades. To the soul trapped inside its body there remaineth no knowledge of the torment the vampyre suffereth in the burning lands deep under the earthe.

I broke off there, too struck to continue. Was my bride being tortured while she slept even now, during the day? The thought was so horrible I near threw down the book and ran to the hole she'd dug. I made myself stop. I rolled another smoke to calm my nerves. It tore at me something fierce, but there was nothing I could do for her now. She'd remember nothing at least, and digging her up would just expose her to the sun, and make sure she remained wherever she was when she slept the day away.

As far as we had guessed, Maria still had her soul because she hadn't actually chosen to be a vampire, or rather, she had accepted what was forced upon her as a sacrifice, willing to offer her immortal soul to save me. She hadn't been controlled by a demon, Maria didn't need to be possessed by a creature from hell to be the feisty, ornery gal I'd come to love.

If she still had her soul, and wasn't under control of some demon that might live in her blood, did she still have to suffer in the pit of Hades while the sun was up? If Maria still had her innocence, did she go to heaven to be with the Good Lord during the daytime? How did this all work? I shut the book; this was beyond my powers of thinkin', my head swam just considering it. I'd read more later, maybe there was some way to cure her of the whole affair.

My hair stood up on the back of my neck of a sudden, I looked up, shielding my eyes against the sun. Something gleamed on the corner of a nearby rooftop. On instinct, I stood up and shifted left, and not a moment too soon.

A shower of splinters sprayed from the bench where I'd been sitting, but no gunshot accompanied it. A little puff of smoke rose from where I'd seen the glint of light on a barrel, but the shooter was gone.

I walked fast down the boardwalk under the awnings, keeping an eye on the rooftops and windows where the last shot had come from. How could they shoot without making a sound? Some kind of sorcery if ever there was one.

I ducked into an alley first chance I got and broke into a run. A bullet kicked up dust right behind my heel at the mouth of the long corridor. The shooter must not have been very practiced at shooting from a high position, or else he was just a bad shot. Small favors and such.

I came out the other end of the alley, and turned right. The sniper, and I hoped there was only one, would have to follow me to get another shot. He missed twice, I didn't think my luck would hold, so I needed to figure out where he'd go, and get there first. There was any number of buildings he could use, but the one I would pick was another three story building, a fancy hotel. Just as I spied it, a man entered the building, walking fast, carrying a long black case. I didn't think clothes were in it.

It was taking a chance, but I ran around to the back of the building, looking for a ladder. It was metal and ran the whole way up the building. I stashed the packages under some empty sacks and crates nearby, and went up the ladder hand over hand as fast as I could.

Just before I reached the top, I heard a door bang shut. I froze, my ears twitching. Someone was moving around on the roof, his boots scraping the grit on the roof as he walked. I tucked my hat into my belt and peered over, just one eye over the ledge. A man knelt against the low wall on the other side of the roof, unlimbering a rifle, and screwing something on to the end of the barrel. The rifle had a long telescope like tube bolted to the top. He laid a bag filled with sand or beans or some such on the ledge and carefully rested the rifle atop it. Then he settled into the gun, sweeping it left and right, no doubt searching for me.

As quietly as I could manage, I stretched my limbs over the ledge and snaked my way over. Staying low, I slipped a Smith loose and kept a bead on the sniper as I approached on cat feet. I put my feet down toe first and then settled my weight, like an injun does when he's walking on dry leaves, and the gritty rooftop didn't make a peep of protest.

I knew the game was up when the sniper's ears pricked, he was fast, but I wasn't playing games. I pulled the trigger as he spun around, my bullet smashing him through the chest. I shot again, the next bullet hitting just above his belt buckle, and my third shot went in just under his collarbone. The rifle dropped from his hands unfired, and he fell back against the ledge, then went over.

I rushed to the edge, just as the sniper hit the ground, dead. A gaggle of passersby looked from the body up the roof where I stood like an idiot.

"Hey, it's that fella' what caused the ruckus yesterday! Call the police!"

"Police! Police!"

In seconds I was sliding down the ladder, my boots on either side of the railing. I hit the ground at a run, snatching my packages out of the garbage as I went.

"Down this alley men, we've got him now!"

Hearing the voices coming up the alley, I had to turn and run back down past the ladder to the other end.

"There he is!" A policeman exclaimed, and I heard a shot a second later. I felt the bullet whiz past, and ducked my head down a few inches, and fired a few shots behind me without looking. A rattled man generally doesn't shoot so well, and I didn't know of anything what rattled a man better than bullets coming back at him. Chunks of brick flew as bullets struck the corner a heartbeat after I rounded it.

I ran hard up the next street, past a familiar figure.

"You're looking worster than the last time I saw yuh," Drawled that familiar drunken voice.

"Jeremiah, I've got men chasing me. Care to lend a hand?"

"Sure," the old rebel grinned, "But you're lookin' worse than the last time I saw yuh. Have you some of this, keeps me nice and strong."

I waved away the proffered bottle and tossed Jeremiah a few dollars from my dwindling stash. I didn't have a clue what to do, but I figured the old rebel would come up with something good.

The police rounded the corner, racing up the street after me. I ducked as another shot split the air; these men were awful careless with their bullets. Passersby dove for cover.

I chanced a look back just in time to see Jeremiah stick his stump out with the long wooden plank strapped to it. The police crashed into it, one man tripped, and then two other tripped over him. Another second and they all went down in a heap. Jeremiah guffawed, and hobbled off, taking nips of his bottle. Money well spent.

I ducked into another alley while the police was all tied up, and then spent the better part of an hour working my way through Memphis and staying as out of sight as a body can in a city like that.

I huddled behind a pile of garbage behind a saloon, tryin' to catch my breath. I was never a fast runner, but I could run flat out for a long time. Maybe it was whatever condition I was developing, but I thought I left my wind a few streets back, and it was taking its time catching up to me.

My head swam for a moment and I felt dizzy. My veins blackened and stood out again, perhaps the drops wore off from all the exertion. I fumbled for the bottle, managed to take the cap off, and then promptly dropped it in the dust as my stomach tried to turn inside out and escape my insides all at the same time.

Vomiting blood into the garbage next to me, I went down on hands and knees, my stomach heaving in great rolling waves.

"That's your life leaving you know, one bit at a time. Your body is purging itself of life."

I looked up startled, I hadn't heard anyone approach over the sounds my insides was making.

A well turned out man stood above me, his white fingers gripping a brass headed cane.

Panicking, I dug out one of the pistols, tried to raise it.

The gun wavered.

"Oh no, none of that now," a cultured voice warned, just before that brass headed cane came crashing down between my eyes.

CHAPTER 14

"I'm surprised you made it this far. It's a good thing I found you."

The man speaking was the same slicked up fella what knocked me over the noggin with the cane. Even though it hadn't worked out so well for me the last time, I felt for my guns. They were gone.

"No reason to fear, take your guns if it makes you feel better. They're unloaded, but if I wished you harm they would do you no good, loaded or not."

"There's a few dead vamps might beg to differ with you," I said as he tossed me the guns. My head hurt like the blazes, but I could clearly see the signs. He was a vampire. I didn't even need to see the fangs to know. Question was, how was he up and walking about it daylight?

"Where is your maker? Surely he should know better than to leave his familiar to the tender mercies of the sun at this late stage? Or perhaps not. You could hardly be more than a few hours from turning. Trust me, when that happens, you do not wish to be out under the sun."

"What are you jawin' about?" My head felt half busted, my mouth was dry, and my skin felt like it was crawling.

"Can it be you are unaware of your condition? Surely not. Tell me true friend, do you know what has befallen you?"

"All I know is I feel like yesterday's garbage."

The stranger nodded, "And smell like it too. Forgive my lack of courtesy. I am Nathaniel Ravenstone, formerly of Europe and the Isles, lately of the Mississippi in its glorious entirety. I have not had the honor of meeting your master, though-"

"I don't have no master," I growled, sitting up. My hands looked gray and wrinkled, thick black veins bulged against the skin. I could feel my heartbeat pounding in my head, the beats were sluggish and loud in my ears.

"You are a familiar. A familiar must have a master. Who gave you the blood?"

"Why should I tell you anything?"

"You needn't say a word, if that is your wish. I have precious little company, most vampires won't come north of Louisiana. Of late our most dangerous enemies prowl the streets, I myself seldom go out at night, strange though that may seem. But I've run into their ilk before. I can certainly understand your reticence to speak of your master, perhaps you were commanded to refrain from doing so. No matter, your secrets are your own. I do wish you would carry a warning to your sire though, when he arises. If he is as unfamiliar with the Order of Saint Michael as he is careless with his familiars, he would do wise to leave Memphis for safer environs."

"I told you, I ain't got no master, or no sire neither. I'm a free American, no one tells me what to do."

Ravenstone chuckled, "Clearly you've yet to be married. I was married once, long ago. When I was turned, I left her, and all my worldly concerns behind for some time. I suppose it was all just as well, she's long since dead, and all I could have done was to watch her grow old and wither and die. She never would have consented to the dark gift. Always so worried about her immortal soul. Perhaps she is the reason I now care so much about regaining mine."

"Not all vampires lose them," I began, then shut my big mouth. I didn't know who this feller was. He might not mean me any harm, but I had no reason to trust him neither.

"Ah, so you're not completely ignorant after all. In fact, quite the opposite. Most vampires, to say nothing of their mortal servants, in whatever stage, know a vampire may regain their soul, and in the rarest of cases, become a child of night without ever losing it. There's always the thirst, and the demon rages, but the condition of one such is much preferable to the state of your average Nosferatu, as we used to refer to ourselves. If you cannot answer I understand, but please, was your master born to darkness with his soul intact, or did he have to regain it?"

"How's about you share first, since you want to flap your beater. How does a critter like you walk around in the daytime? Shouldn't you be lying dead in the ground somewhere?"

Ravencroft steepled his hands under his chin, looking thoughtful for a moment before answering.

"For many years, I did just as you said, and was blissfully none the wiser as to what went on while I slumbered. You may not know this, and perhaps you are better off not knowing, but since you shall be in a state such as I am before long, I feel I should tell you. Ignorance can be bliss, until the day comes when you eventually realize your state, and then it feels like a caul ripped from a wound you didn't even know was there. Seeing that book in your possession, the history of our kind, makes me think you know more than you seem to let on. No matter, I grow lonely these days, and since they may soon come to a close, one way or another, and you have no business being out in the sun, perhaps my story will enlighten you to the darkness you shall dwell in the rest of your days.

Many, many years ago, when I chose to be turned, I embraced being a vampire and all it entailed. Indeed there was no choice. Some say the soul leaves the body entirely, or that only a tether remains. But in choosing the dark gift, one in effect chooses evil, the demon binds itself to your soul and lives in the blood, and we are but darker versions of ourselves. Or so is my way of thinking today. I was happy enough, as I would have called it then, feasting on blood and innocent life with abandon. I was brought up in a very tra-

ditional coven, we believed ourselves servants of Satan, the
natural enemies of mankind, and so we comported ourselves.
We kept familiars, such as you are, they guarded our graves
in the daylight hours, obeyed out commands without question, unable to refuse orders, all due to the small amounts of
blood given to our willing servants.

They were disgusting creatures, as I looked at them then,
subsisting on bugs and the crawling creatures of the earth,
vermin eating vermin. Trapped between death and life...but
you already know how it works. If they were injured or in
ill health when we took them in, they only lasted for weeks,
sometimes days. We made a point in only choosing the
healthiest and strongest humans for our servants, but inevita-
bly they came to look such as you do now, hideous and skel-
etal, appearing more deathly than we, their undead masters.

For loyal service they were rewarded, for failure we
destroyed them before they could turn. Vampires do not kill
our own kind, this is our oldest, and perhaps our only law. It
is rarely broken.

As I said, I was content to serve the devil himself, thinking in my wicked heart I was free of all punishment, I would
walk the earth and never know the torments of hell as other
wicked souls, not until the end of time and even then, we
thought we would play a crucial part in the final war against
God, and win our freedom to rule the new earth for time
beyond time.

I was always a curious sort, and shortly set out to become
something of a historian of our race, at least among our
coven. My own was one of the oldest and most powerful in
the old world, and we moved from castle to manor to estate,
I spent my nights reading tomes of lore from the beginning
of time, learning long dead languages of forgotten civilizations to do so.

So fascinated was I by this window to the past that I even
left off feeding, taking nourishment only when my fellow
vampires grew concerned and brought me a tender maiden

or a strapping young man in the flower of youth. Most of what I read was mere myths and folk tales, primitive superstitions, but here and there was a bit of real knowledge. I began to seek out the deeper magicks of our world, but the greatest of them is this: Only death can pay for life.

The most horrifying reality I discovered was that while we thought ourselves aslumber in our graves by day, our souls underwent unimaginable agony in hell. When the sun sets we rise, the torment we suffer utterly forgotten, a cycle to be repeated for as long as we walk the earth in unlife. The very idea floored me, soon I was so tormented by this discovery I could find no pleasure in the night, just thinking that I would soon suffer the pains of death and hell when the sun rose again. I would have met the sun if I thought it would help, but that would only mean fully aware and never ending suffering.

In an ancient book I found in a monastery in the heart of the Levant, I discovered a spell which would have been utterly forbidden, even among our kind if anyone had still been aware it existed. It was designed for one purpose, to break the part of our curse that caused us to forget our suffering. With great dread and anticipation, I set about obtaining the particulars I required to work the magick. The details are unimportant; neither would I share them with any soul, living or undead. In my youthful ignorance I had supposed to only be aware of the one day in hell, imagine my surprise when I not only experienced and remembered the agony I suffered under the sun and below it, but did so the next night, and the night after that. And every night since, until I found a rumor of a great treasure, thought of as a fairytale and a myth among our kind.

For a vampire to walk during the day is a fantasy, an impossible dream, all vampires want it, but we are told by the oldest of our kind, as they were told themselves in turn, that such is a myth, we are meant to spend our days still and helpless, it is the unavoidable condition of our race. Men do not seek that which they believe not to exist.

I would not hear such things; I sought and sought the world over, conscious of every day spent in that place of torment. My sanity was hanging by a thread, I poured out my rage and helplessness on countless innocent souls, I feasted on blood, but it was all ash in my mouth. There was only dread of the sun going down, and what would come soon after.

I searched the world over for years, desiring oblivion, if I could find it. I continued my search for a solution to my suffering, surely there must be hope, I had to believe that.

Deep in the Himalayas, I climbed to a high peak, its very existence merely rumors and echoes. There I found what I sought. The price of obtaining it was almost higher than I could bear, but my awareness of the suffering I felt by day gave me the strength to endure what was needed. My mind nearly broken, I emerged from the cave after three days with what I had sought. I have not spent another day in hell since. I was able to walk in the day, no longer needing to rest in the earth. The sun no longer had any terrors for me.

I returned to my coven, but things were not the same. I could not help but feel superior, and at the same time, pitying the poor damned souls who slept by day in their graves deep below the cities of man, unaware of just how they spent the hours. I dared not tell of it, nor to reveal I had discovered the secret of walking in the light. The older ones would have killed me instantly and taken what was mine, the younger ones would have tried with all their power.

I thought myself wise, but I was still young and foolish in my ways. For a week upon my return I pretended to sleep in my coffin, afraid my secret would be revealed. Soon, the temptation grew too great, and I walked among my countrymen under the sun, reveling in the life they lived under the shining sun. Drunk on new life and gallons of hot salty blood, I returned to my crypt before sunset. The familiars we kept saw me enter, bowing low in obeisance. I could not command their silence, they were not my own, the blood they'd had was from another. I slew them one and all to keep my secret.

There was no way to explain their deaths, and I found I had no desire to return to hiding in my grave by day. I fled, but I was pursued by my own kind. One by one I destroyed them breaking the only law of God or man left to me. The older ones I dragged into the sun while they slept, they never woke up from their hellish dreams. The younger ones fled from me then, but I hunted them down and littered the earth with their ashes. This was only my own coven, I did not wish to destroy any whose destruction upon which my own survival did not depend.

I wandered the earth, visiting coven after coven until I realized I no longer sought the company of my own kind. Knowing what torments they suffered made it seem like the dark and daring life we all thought we lived was but a farce. Instead of feeling immortal or invincible I was reduced to a fearful and cringing creature of the night, having the taste of hell still fresh in my mouth. Soon, I came to realize we were being played for fools. I do not know if we are indeed servants of satin or if he even cares for us in some small way, but I do know the dark gift that was offered is nothing but a curse, we undergo torment all the same, a fate which we might have averted had we lived. It is little wonder he is called the father of lies.

I began to search desperately for some way to remove the curse, to become mortal again, vowing to recompense for my past wrongs. I sought out the church, posed as a man, studied the writings which had all the answers the most ancient texts I had read only hinted at: Only death could pay for life.

But these answers were not enough for me in my present condition, I was convinced the church held deeper mysteries, ones they hid away in their most secret places. I traveled to Rome, to the Vatican, there I would find the answers I sought. I lived in the archives, using all my skill and power to remain unobserved, sitting in the high places and low, poring over tome after tome of their most closely guarded knowledge. I only satisfied my thirst when I was driven mad with hunger, and then only on the evildoer, even then it was almost unbearable the thought of sending a soul to that place of torment where I had been myself.

I learned they had priests of an order which hunted those such as I was, warriors of God, sworn to give their lives in the fight against all manner of evil. I took even more care to go unnoticed, but not having to spend the days helpless to any man with a torch or a stake, I was confident I had nothing to fear.

That was when he found me. A vampire much older than I was. Jude, he was called then. He was a Roman by birth and in unlife, older than I by far, one of the elders of our kind, though I had never heard of him. He was so old he remembered the great coliseum of the city, having been placed in it under a sentence of death for breaking an ancient law, against being a disciple of Christ.

He had been left strapped to a pillar, a tall and strong young man, a soldier in the Roman army, a legionnaire. Once he was found out and seized under Emperor Nero's reign, in the great persecutions thereof. His fellow prisoners had been content to die, offering no resistance, singing hymns and praises to their God. Jude, for such was the name he had taken when he became a Christian, had been born and bred a Roman soldier, and could not stomach the thought of peaceful submission to death, despite his beliefs. Using his great strength, he broke free of his bonds and fetched up a spear left carelessly about during the intermezzo, they would play music while the arena was cleared after the gladiatorial combats, and prisoners would be executed while they prepared for more carnage afterwards.

Jude wielded the spear with an unreal strength, and against all odds slew two of the lions before the rest savaged him terribly. He clung to life, and was dragged from the arena and tossed in a mass grave, forgotten, left uncovered until the conclusion of the games.

A passing vampire heard whispers of the courage he had shown, and sought him out where he lay at death's door in the pit filled with corpses of the slain. Vampires only offer the blood to the beautiful and courageous. The vampire offered him the dark gift, and the thought of death had sunk well into Jude's mind, and his courage failed him. He accepted.

Later, when he fully understood the curse he had wrought upon himself, he slew his maker, binding him to a great funeral pyre and setting it alight, sending him to the hell wherein he had damned his progeny. So great was Jude's strength of will that he fought back against the demon in his blood, resisting with all his might the desire to feed, spending his nights praying and crying out to God for forgiveness in the churches.

When I met him, he had been about to embark on a plan I considered folly, but he could not do it alone. Jude was convinced he could bring his demon into submission by sheer force of will and penitential suffering.

I sought the same cure he did, but by different means. I hoped to find some long hidden secret to reclaiming my soul from the brink of hell; Jude sought to take it back by force. He wanted me to burn him to the point of death, again and again, and by this to cause the demon in his blood to flee.

The first night, I burned him badly, but when I extinguished the flames, he cried for more. He refused to take blood, and I refused to continue. I was certain he would burn too far, and his soul would be trapped in hell forever. Jude was determined that his will should defeat the demon's until it should leave him in peace to live out a mortal life in penitence.

It was in vain that I pleaded, and so the next night I burned him again, and again after that, stopping just short of ending his unnatural existence on the earth. Jude was locked in a battle of wills, a battle for his soul.

In the end, it was not enough, the demon grew weaker, but did not leave him, nor did the thirst for blood. Jude then pleaded for my help with an even more daring plan, one I thought was madness.

I ignored his pleas for a time, and nursed Jude back to health. I obtained small quantities of blood from the prostitutes and destitute denizens of that great and rotten city, which I forced upon him.

Still, Jude's great force of will eroded my resistance, and eventually I relented, convinced though I was this would be the end of the one creature on this earth that was like me. I made the necessary preparations while Jude spent the day in hell, dead to the world.

One last time I tried to talk him out of this brave but foolhardy plan, it smacked of hubris to me. And hubris is always punished.

Jude was resolute, he would succeed now or spend eternity in hell, rightfully suffering for his abandonment of his faith and the sins he had committed, I could not imagine accepting such a fate. But then, I had tasted it, and Jude had only the idea of it he had gleaned from the scriptures and teachings of the church. I remembered one line that said something to the effect of how no one knows or can comprehend what God has prepared for them that love Him, all I could dwell upon was that I knew very well what He had prepared for them that defied Him.

I argued in vain. Jude's will was stronger than mine, stronger than any man I have ever met, living or undead.

Deep in the caverns of the most closely guarded archives in the world, Jude and I made our way like shadows into the deepest depths. In that lonely sanctuary, not one man in a decade made the journey to the nearly forgotten room at the bottom.

The walls were lined with books in languages I perhaps alone had learned in my travels, from civilizations long dead and thankfully forgotten. The floor of the room housed a large pool of holy water, running from a font which used to be an ancient part of the catacombs, where Christians had come to baptize in secret, during the persecutions of millennia past. In the middle of that font rose a statue, great and tall, of the whitest marble. The archangel Michael loomed over us, his mien fierce, the holy warrior angel of God. He was just a statue, but so masterfully sculptured by an unknown hand that I half feared he would smite us the next moment with heavenly wrath.

I would set Jude aflame, and as the fire cleansed the sin and the demon from his corporeal form, I would push him into the holy water, and this would destroy his body and complete the cleansing of his soul. Suicide was a mortal sin, as Jude believed, and so he would need me to murder him, my only friend left in the world. I was seeking my own redemption after a fashion, but in different ways, and I had a multitude of sins to my account, what harm could one more do me, especially if it was meant for the good? Still, I was convinced I was sending him straight to hell, to burn forever in a pool of flame.

Once again, I balked. Jude convinced me in the end by the sheer power of his will and his own belief. He reasoned that if the demon could animate the dead tissue of a corpse, was that so different from giving the twisted specimen of life we endured to a form made of a different material? By Jude's reasoning, he would will himself into the statue, and inhabit it, the thirst that remained and even grew when he was burned would be unable to satisfy itself in a body made of stone. He would will himself at the moment of death into the marble, and there begin his new life, and his new path. In this way he would starve the demon, and be freed from the thirst.

It was insane, but there was no resisting. Jude prayed, his eyes closed, his cursed lips smouldered as the words of a psalm rolled off his lips. I covered him in oil, and lit the torch. There would be no extinguishing the flames this time. He had insisted.

I lit the torch with great care, for I had no wish to burn and our kind is notoriously susceptible to the flames. A tear of blood rolled down one cheek as I said farewell and set my only friend aflame.

He screamed in agony, the wailing could no doubt be heard throughout the archives floors above, even the holy city would wonder at the sound. This I all learned later. When he blackened in the flames, I shoved him with the burning stick in my hand and he fell into the pool in a sizzling cloud of steam. The fire was extinguished, but now undead flesh smoked and bubbled in the holy water, the steam blocked the view, the heat drove me back.

After some time the air cleared, though the burning stench of flesh remained.

The pool was defiled, blackened, nothing left but ashes on water. I shed another tear. Jude was gone.

I closed my eyes, trying to stop myself from imagining the torment Jude would already be enduring. I wondered if he would blame me for his failure. Jude was stronger than I was, I could never go to the lengths he had gone to for his attempt at salvation. I had no doubt then that someday I would see him in that infernal pit, and I could ask him myself.

A sudden groan of stone sliding on stone sent my eyes fluttering open. I wiped away the bloody tears to see the great marble statue of the archangel looming over me. It took a step off the pedestal, into the murky waters. It had worked!

I stared in awe as he approached. My friend was inside! He was right!

The Archangel of heaven stood over me, his wings spread wide, covering me in their shadow.

"Jude?"

"No," His voice boomed, echoing through the chamber, "Michael. And the time for judgment has come for all our kind!"

120

CHAPTER 15

I fled, with vampiric speed, up through the archives, and through the city, heedless of whoever saw the blur running at speed through their mortal world heedless of discovery. There was only one thing I feared now.

Michael pursued me on great stone wings, some supernatural force worked by the demonic spirit now entwined with his enabled him to take flight for all his bulk. I was faster than any mortal or animal, but Michael was faster still. He caught me near the Tiber, cutting off my retreat.

"Jude! Don't do this! I am your friend!" I protested as he trod the ground with marble feet, cracking the paving stones underneath his great weight.

"I have no friends. Only a mission of vengeance. Vengeance for all the innocent blood spilled by our cursed race," Jude paused, and somehow his marble face grew even harder, "Your race."

"How did you escape?" I broke in.

Ravenstone smiled, "I didn't. A moment later "Michael" sliced me in half with a blow from one of his great wings, and both halves of me flew into the river. I was pulled along in the current, just managing to grab a hold of my lower half, and pulled myself together. I let the current take me until I settled to the bottom. It took a day and a half, but my grievous wound mended, and the sun was one thing I need not have feared.

At sunrise I pulled myself from the Tiber, whole, and drank my fill of the first human I found. I passed through the city, expecting winged vengeance to come swooping down from the heavens on me any moment. But as I passed through the city, a throng of onlookers drew my attention.

There in the middle of the piazza where Saint Peter met his end, was a statue of the archangel Michael, sans spear, posed to the amazement of all the people of Rome, the crowd exclaiming that it was a miracle, a gift from heaven.

The gift from heaven still must slumber by day, or so it seemed, but the marble did not burn in the sun as his flesh would have. He merely became a statue again, while his soul burned in hell. To this day I do not know if he is aware of this, but I never told him, and still would not. He may have tried to kill me, but he was my only friend. I tell you now only because I have lived long upon the earth and am lonely and separated from my kind, which you will soon become. Pass my warnings along to the one who made you, and beware. I have seen the statue Michael, who was once my friend, here on display just this past day. There were pieces of him missing, and that I cannot explain, but I know he will never stop. His will is unbreakable; he has no mercy, pity, or compassion for our kind. Come nightfall, do your best to flee."

Ravenstone looked wistfully out the window at the dying light for a time.

"I appreciate the yarn," I said, buckling on the gun belt, "No hard feelin's about the rap on the head neither. Thanks for the advice."

"You should not leave while there is light in the sky. I have seen this a thousand times. You are very close to death now. It simply won't do to have you rise again while the sun is still up. The results are not...optimal."

"Much obliged, but I'll be going just the same."

Ravenstone sighed.

"Here, if you won't listen to your elders, at least take this with you."

He held out an amulet, steel woven in a knot, some kind of writing or markings covering it.

"What's that?"

"This is the secret of walking in the sun. After tomorrow night, I shall need it no longer, one way or the other. I am about to embark on a course of action that shall lead to my salvation from the curse I have borne so long, and which you are just beginning with. A unique opportunity, if you will. That is why I am here in this city. Before the sun comes up on that night, I shall either be cured of my affliction, or cease to exist entirely. In all, either outcome saves me from an eternity in torment, I have existed long enough it makes no matter what else happens."

"Are you sure about this? Won't you-"

"Burn? Yes. Perhaps one more day in the flames is what I deserve. If I am successful, it can only serve to advance my redemption. I have a multitude of sins to atone for. I have managed to gain some measure of control over my demon and the thirst, but I have not been entirely success- ful. In all the years I have walked this earth, only two truths have I learned: Only death can pay for life, and the thirst...it always wins."

I tipped back my hat and scratched my head, I was feelin' awful itchy.

"Ain't you ever tried askin' for forgiveness?" I hadn't done a sight of readin' in the good book, but from what little I knew, that seemed to be the gist of it.

Ravenstone smiled at me like I was some snot-nosed kid.

"A nice sentiment, but I cannot believe forgiveness could be so simple for one such as I."

"Well, best of luck then, with your redemption and all," I tipped my hat again and left.

For all I knew, that bit about the amulet could be mere snake oil and hogwash, but I put it on just the same. If what he said was true, no good would come of burning up until I could put this piece of jewelry on Maria. It would look bet- ter on her anyway, and I valued her life more than my own.

So I was to become a vampire. I didn't choose it, so I hoped it meant I wasn't damned from the get-go. On the other hand Maria wouldn't have to carry me around any-more, so I could take the good along with the bad.

Suddenly, my heart started beating loud and fast, the blood rushed in my ears. My nerves shot aflame with pure pain. A great torrent of blood rushed out of my mouth in a flood, and I felt my knees hit the ground.

I struggled back to my feet, the beats of my ticker came slower now, a few ragged breaths between each pump.

Thump-thump.

I struggled for each step.

Thump-thump.

I stumbled into an alleyway, choked with human waste and rotting garbage.

Thump-thump.

It was happening. I was dying.

Thump-thump.

Not here, anywhere but a manure soaked alley in Mem-phis.

Thump-thump.

I was looking up at the sky, the packages wrapped in old rags lay next to me, the dying rays of the sun stretched over the clouds in the sky in a shower of pink and purple, like a painting of heaven I'd seen in a barroom in the New Mexico territory.

Thump-th-

Maria.

CHAPTER 16

"**He's** dead, but there's no marks on 'im. Curious..."

"Look at his face, all sunk in like that, he looks like he's been dead a while. Smells like it too."

"Let's just go through his pockets. If'n we're lucky, no one else has found him yet."

"He's carrying some serious weaponry on him. We can get a few dollars for these."

"Say, what's this, a belly band full of dollars and gold pieces!"

"Take it and let's go, I hear someone coming."

I heard the sounds as if far away. Slowly, I started feeling my fingers, then my toes, but I couldn't move or open my eyes.

"What's this?"

"Just another corpse Bill, let's move along, the meat wagon'll go around in the morning and collect 'em. You want to spend all night askin' folks if they seen somethin' out of the ordinary? Just another no account drifter by the looks of 'im. Fell afoul of the wrong feller, or welched on a bet, most like. We'll see three more before the patrol's over. Let's go down by the waterfront, the gals is always out there."

"You and them gals, all you ever do is look. Say, shine that lantern over here. It is, it's that fella' what stepped all over the chief! Whats-his-name..."

"Wilder. Clefford or Clyde I think."

No, it was Clay. Clay Wilder. Supposed to be a real bad hombre from out west, the newspapers used to write stories about him. I read some crazy yarn a few months back about somethin' he was supposed to have done south of the border. Real wild stuff."

"You got to quit readin' that garbage Frank. I'm tellin' you, it'll rot your brain. Not that it's good for much anyway. Some bad hombre from out west, huh. Prob'ly shoulda' stayed there, looks like Memphis was too much for 'im. Serves him right. There's two of our men dead on account of this low-life. Sergeant Williams'll recover, they say, but his leg is shot, heck, literally. Come on, let's go tell the station, we'll get the credit for it."

"Say, how dead you think he looks anyway? You think it's been long?"

"What're you gettin' after?"

"We put a bullet in him see? Make it look like we chased him down. We'll be heroes, and prob'ly get promotified to boot! The Chief wants this feller bad. No one'll ask no questions."

"Say, that's not the worstest ideer you've had..."

"I'm gonna plug 'im."

"The hell you is! I'm gonna' plug him!"

"Okay, okay, lookee here, we both put a bullet in him, and we both share the credit."

"Alright, that'll work for me. We saw the criminal, chased him down this alley, and he turned on us, blazin' away, and we shot 'im deader'n a possum."

"Don't say that, it's all wrong, possums only play dead."

"What's yer point?! They die too, for real sometimes. He's just one of the ones what's really dead."

I flexed my fingers, just a little. I managed to raise one eyelid, just a hair. The last of the light disappeared from the sky above.

Twin hammers clicked as they was thumbed back. My eyes flew open.

"Aw shucks, he ain't dead, he was just drunk or somethin'!"

"He was too dead, and wasnt playin' no possum neither.

He wasn't breathin'!"

"Well, let's just fix that little problem, and then we don't have to tell no tales, we'll shoot him fair and square."

The guns fired, but I was no longer there. Two bullets sparked off the pavement where I'd laid.

"Evening officers," I drawled, tipping my hat. I felt like a million bucks.

The two policemen turned aghast, their eyes wide. I balled up a fist and let one of them have it, right in the mouth. My hand was filled with gore a second later, my fist had gone right through the back of his head!

"Oh stars! It's true what they wrote! You was fightin' vampires, and now you is one!"

I grinned, and took a step towards the man what tried to kill me.

"Get back you foul creature of the night! I'll do to you what you did to them mex vampers, I swear it! You stay back now!"

The man backed away, firing shot after shot.

The bullets hurt a bit, but not so bad as when I was mortal, I guess on account of the fact that I used to be quite susceptible to dyin' from 'em. The wounds started to close instantly.

My stomach growled. I didn't want no flapjacks, and thank heavens, if I could still do that, no spiders or cockroaches neither. There was only one thing I hungered for, thirsted for, and it was right in front of me.

My fangs sank deep, the policeman's skinny, weak arms beat uselessly against my back as the hot blood poured into my mouth. It was a taste of heaven. The body went limp in my arms, I'd drained him dry in less than a minute.

Perhaps I should have felt guilty at what I'd done, or even just a mite sheepish, but I was feelin' better'n a buck during the fall rut surrounded by does.

Blood was better than any meal I'd ever tasted, more heady than the strongest moonshine. I would just do as Maria had done, and prey on those who sought to prey on me. I was killin' folks right and left the day long anyhow, what did it matter if I also got my meals at the same time?

As good as it was I wouldn't have wished for it. It just didn't seem natural. I reckoned that's because it wasn't. An abomination, a mockery of life, something never intended to be. But I didn't feel much like pondering; I had something to do, and Maria would be up and about real soon, if not already.

"Clay?"

I whirled, so fast I nearly spun myself too far over, but caught my balance easily. This vampire stuff took a little gettin' used to.

Maria had appeared in a flash.

"How'd you find me?" I grinned at her.

"Oh Clay, is it true? I could sense you, as soon as I awoke, I could feel where you were, what you were! Clay, please believe me, I never meant for this to happen!"

I gathered her in my arms.

"Don't fret darlin', I think it's alright, I'm the same as you are. But stars, the thirst! How d'you put up with it?"

Maria wiped away a tear and sniffled up at me.

"I didn't...I didn't want to disappoint you!"

"Darlin' you could never, ever disappoint me. Not if we walk this earth a million years. Not if'n we walked this earth a...not ever!"

We hugged and laughed and strolled through the night, me carrying my packages wrapped in rags. They looked like just more garbage so thankfully the thieves hadn't taken them. My money belt was gone, taken by the thieves, through precious little was left for them to have. I guess you really can't take it with you after all. I told Maria, all about my little visit with Ravenstone, the origins of our adversary who posed as the archangel of heaven, and the amulet I draped over Maria. She would never need fear the sun again, and if one of us did end up spending their days suffering in some place of torment after all, I'd rather it be me. At least I wouldn't remember it.

Everything looked different. Instead of the night bein' gloomy and dark, it was no harder to see than the daytime, heck, I saw even farther and sharper and clearer. I'd be able to shoot the wings off a gnat at a hundred yards or more. I even wished for a moment I was a no-account dirty low-down thievin' rascal again, 'cause I'd steal Maria the moon with my newfound powers.

We'd strolled out of the inhabited quarters of the city into another neighborhood where all that stood was the broken down ramshackle remnants of houses and shops and factories from before the fever had hit.

"So we need to lure Michael to where we want him to be," Maria was saying. "This time, we choose the battleground. With both of us this strong, we've got an even better chance of-"

"Uh, Darlin? Don't look now, but I don't think we get to pick this time neither."

I shoved Maria off to one side and dove on top of her as the white chunk of stone swooped down out of the sky like a bird of prey.

"Here, I got us some presents, spent most of the rest of our cash on 'em, so they better work."

"Clay! You spent all our money on guns?!" Maria shouted.

"Not just guns," I grinned, "though yeah, mostly. Thieves took the rest while I was dead. So at least we got something to show for it."

"What is this?" Maria practically screamed as I finished unwrapping my own package, my eyes riveted on the sky.

"Oh, you've got the wrong one, here, this one's yours!"

I tossed the weapon I'd unwrapped to Maria and she tossed hers to me.

"Lookout!" Maria shouted, this time diving on top of me to avoid a swoop from Michael, his hands and feet dug long furrows in the street as the creosote blocks went shattering and tumbling in all directions.

"What am I supposed to do with this thing?"

"Just point and shoot!"

The weapons gleamed unnaturally in the moonlight. I could only guess at their origin, but Schwab had assured me, no matter what I needed them for, they would prove as effective as any weapon on this earth. They had well better be, for 30 thousand dollars. I figured they was worth even more if they performed as advertised, but I also got that Schwab wasn't in business so much for the money as for the satisfaction of having the best dry goods store on either side of the Mississippi, and that covered some territory. Having all kinds of junk didn't do no one any good unless you used it or sold it. I had been the lucky fella what cornered the market on heavy firepower that day.

The weapon in Maria's hands was long and sleek, four barrels bound together with two barrel bands, an oddly shaped hammer on the back you had to cock before each shot. Schwab had said to be right careful, both with whatever you chose to utterly destroy with it, and with not wasting a shot. He said there wasn't likely anyone left alive that knew how to load it proper, and them wasn't no ordinary bullets, or so I gathered. There was an inscription on the butt stock which read: Thorisdottir. Maria's rifle was covered in twisted scrollwork patters of runes and all manner of design, my own weapon was a mite simpler.

Also covered in that strangely glowing pattern, I held in my hands the thickest hammer I ever did see, inscribed with the word: Thorisen.

"Here he comes again," Maria shouted.

"Get behind me!" I yelled back.

"No Clay, we fight together, remember?!"

"I know gal! Now get behind me and use my shoulder for a rest, we can't afford to miss!"

"Oh...well, alright."

Maria laid that heavy barrel across my shoulder as I stood as still as possible so's she could use me for a rest. She had become quite the shot.

"Steady now!" I warned as the marble hulk in the sky came around for another pass and dove, screaming through the air like a flyin' locomotive, 'cept faster.

"Now!" I breathed and Maria squeezed off a shot. The sound of a thunderclap rang through my ears from inches away, a great bolt of lightning crackled out of the barrel and shot through the sky, striking the stone figure like a bolt from the heavens, just from the other way.

Michael tumbled to the ground.

Maria and I sped to the crater marking the spot where Michael had landed.

He rose slowly from the pit, one wing broken off, glaring at us through gray stone chips of eyes.

"Well, how 'bout that. We got us a fallen angel."

"I think we should welcome him, as you say, good and proper-like."

I stepped aside so the little lady could have her fun. She'd been smacked around some the last time we'd met, it was only fair to let her have some payback.

Maria cocked the hammer and tucked the weapon in her shoulder as Michael stretched up to his full height and stepped up out of the crater.

"Ola Senor!" She barked happily, and yanked the trigger.

Another thunderclap, and a bolt of blue that knocked Michael end over end a stone's throw down the street.

Michael started to rise, and Maria hit him again.

"Bienvenido!" Maria sang merrily, and yanked the trigger a third time.

The next blast hit Michael as he tried to protect himself with his last wing, the sparks and electricity flew everywhere as the wing shattered into a thousand stone pieces, and the living statue was thrown back to the earth.

"And finalmente, Adios!"

Maria pulled the trigger again, and the bricks in the road rattled like bed-slats as the bolt shot out of the rifle loudest of all, throwing Maria on her backside.

A cloud of smoke obscured the statue, Maria climbed to her feet, and we waited for the haze to clear.

The statue strode out of the cloud, missing both wings and half an arm, with a great chunk of stone torn away from his abdomen. His gray stone eyes burned with fury, and glowed molten with rage.

Maria pulled the trigger again, this time without commentary in espanol.

Click.

"Oh, is that all I get?" She looked at me, disappointed.

"Four barrels, four shots, 's about right." I drawled, swinging the hammer back over my shoulder.

"My turn." The hammer was huge, the great flat block at the top glowed eerily in the moonlight, but it felt light as a feather.

I took a hopping step and swung. Michael did the same, but a split second too late.

With the crash of steel on stone, Michael was once again flying, but without wings, skidding and sliding over the pavement. Little crackles of lightning sizzled through the air at the moment of impact; this was no ordinary hammer by a longshot.

I ran after, and as he tried to rise, I smashed him again, my hammer collided with his big fist and the stone shattered in a hundred pieces.

He swung what was left of his other arm at me, bellowing, but I ducked low and whipped the hammer around like it was a hickory stick, striking the business end into his knee with such force that the whole leg shattered.

Michael cried out in rage and frustration, I didn't rightly know if he felt pain at all in his marble body, but it was time we found out.

As the once mighty statue fell to the ground, Maria

rushed in with Thorisdottir and I with Thorisen, and she smashed off his remaining leg with wicked blows while I set about reducing the rest of his body to rubble.

Finally, only his head remained, glaring at us through glowing eyes.

"This ends not here, my work is not yet done!" Michael roared in defiance.

"Oh, ends here it does, friend, it does."

I swung the hammer high and then back down, Maria reversed the rifle and did the same.

We struck at the same instant, and the glowering face disappeared into mere chips of broken marble.

Maria slumped into me; I put my arm around her shoulder.

"You and me gal, together, ain't nothin' we can't lick."

"Yes, but I think...I could take you!" Maria shouted playfully, and threw her best punch to my stomach.

She backed away, a smile on her luscious lips.

"Oh gal, you done it now..." I teased back, easing back my hat.

"Think you can catch me?" Maria blurred and ran off up the street.

"Think?! Hell! I know I can!" I raced after her.

We chased each other in the moonlight, back and forth until we were well out of town and into the woods. We frolicked under the stars and the night sky. I tossed her in a lake, then she snuck up on me and sent me flying head over heels with a well placed blow from a fallen tree.

When dawn approached we dug a deep hole out there in the woods, miles away from Memphis. The steeldust caught up to us just before dawn, and jumped onto his back in the hole.

"Wait, how do we cover it up? If you and me and the horse are all-"

"You gave me the amulet, remember Clay? I haven't seen the sunrise in so long, and I thought I'd never see it again. You never know how much you miss things like that until you do. Sleep now, my love, and I will see you at dusk. I want to sit in the sun and just feel it on my face again."

I nodded. I'd seen my fill of sunrises all throughout my life, but I figured sooner or later I'd learn to miss them all the same.

"You won't do nothin' foolish?"

Maria nodded.

"You'll stay out of trouble?"

She nodded again.

"Alright, just don't go thinkin' you're invincible just on account of that there necklace. Michael might be gone, and it might mean the order packs up and heads for greener pasture, and it might not. I'd rather know you were safe until we know what's what. You stay out of town, y'hear?"

"I'lll be perfectly safe husband." Maria said in her sweetest voice.

I must have got suckered in by her honeyed tones, because just as she started fillin in the dirt, I realized what words she'd used. She said she'd be safe, and that she wouldn't do anything foolish, not that she'd stay out of town. Then I thought about how well I'd listened to that advice when it had been her goin' in the hole.

"Maghmphflfl!" I started to call out as my mouth filled with dirt.

The sun must have broke the horizon then, because I felt myself go limp, and then there was nothing.

Chapter 17

I burst from the grave, a sudden uncontrollable spasm running through my nerves and sinews which shook the soil from my clothes and left me standing above the hole in the earth clean as a whistle.

All that was ruined a moment later when the steeldust copied my act, showering me with a fresh layer of grave dirt.

"Thanks a lot mule!" I snorted.

The steeldust snorted back, and started cropping grass. He left off it after a moment, spitting the green shoots out like they was the worst-tasting stuff in the world. He did it most mornings, I guess as smart as he was he still woke up forgetting he was a vampire horse, and grass just wasn't gonna' cut it no more.

"Maria?"

I heard no answer, could not sense her near. There was something though, like a slight tug on my senses, pulling me in a direction, and I knew in the back of my head it was where she even now.

I couldn't be mad, I'd done the same thing more'n once. Well, I could be mad, on account of bein' that I was mad regardless.

"Come on, we need to ride," I said to the horse. I was plenty fast now, but he was even faster.

We reached Memphis is no time flat. I hopped off, and gave the steeldust a smack on the rump. He needed to feed, and it wouldn't do to be tearing through the town on an undead horse, that kind of thing seemed like to give me some unwanted attention.

I just needed to get in and find Maria and get out again.

I walked the streets, following that little tug in my head the same way Maria must have done to find me last night. Before long, I became aware of other things.

The sights and sounds, the smells all combined in such a way that alerted me. I listened hard, sorting through the footsteps in my mind. When I concentrated, I could close in on a set, and I noticed I kept hearing the same ones again and again, following me through the streets turn after turn.

When the wind shifted, I could smell them. Leather and cloth and sweat, same as most others. What set them apart was oil and metal. Not the common smell of gun oil and blued steel, but olive oil and silvered blades.

I was being followed already, they had picked me up. Just how many of these fellers were there anyway?

The order needed to be dealt with, but finding Maria was much more important. If they attacked, I would have no choice but to make them regret it, but for now I could only follow the tug in my head.

Another option soon presented itself. I was no longer a mere man, but a vampire. I was faster and stronger now, and the order might not even be aware of my change. I ducked behind a fast moving carriage, and quick as a flash, rolled under and grabbed hold of the axles, using my newfound strength to cling tight to the smooth metal underneath.

The carriage was going the same place I was, so I went along for the ride, doing my best to avoid the piles of manure in the streets. I mostly suceeded.

I was getting closer, the pull of Maria's presence grew stronger. We were along the waterfront now. I dropped from the carriage and slipped into an alley. Building a smoke, I merely listened for a while. Something told me Maria was very close, but I waited. Surely if she could have she would have been waiting for me to arise at sundown, if she was still here along the waterfront she might be in trouble. She had been taken from me before, I was not about to walk into an ambush and be taken unawares.

I closed my eyes, listening to the rough talk and sounds of the waterfront. I walked some, looking for any signs of the order's presence, but found none. Soon it was apparent from the direction of the pull that Maria was on one of the vessels lining the waterfront.

It didn't take long to sort out which boat it was. A side-wheel model, a floating palace, one of the largest steamboats I've ever seen. Gold tracings lined the walkways and walls of the giant vessel; it was a picture of opulence. Told you I was learning some new words.

Warily, I approached the vessel. I was unarmed save my derringer, the one gun the thieves what looted my corpse hadn't been diligent enough to find.

"Mr. Wilder! So glad you could attend! The master will be most pleased you have arrived. Come with me, if you please."

"I'm not here for cards, Merely, where's my wife?" The servant who'd brought my wagon to the graveyard smiled with his teeth but not his eyes. He was wearing evening attire, like a fella might do attending a grand ball.

"The lovely Mrs. Wilder awaits you within sir, we've been keeping her comfortable and entertained. Master Icarus is most determined none shall ever have cause to complain of our...hospitality. This way..."

Merely walked up the gangway, and there was little I could do but follow. Maria's presence was very near. When the wind blew, I could catch the traces of her scent. She was indeed aboard the ship. I walked up the long steps to the ship, the river swirling past underneath me. When Merely had his back turned, I slipped the derringer up my sleeve. If this was a trick, there would be blood on the Mississippi tonight.

I followed Merely down the side of the wheel boat, and into a real fancy lounge decorated with small Greek statues and paintings what looked like they came from scenes in the Bible. We went through that room and down a long walk-

137

way, passing paintings of a lush landscape with a man and a woman reclining under trees I never seen before, another with a woman picking an apple from a tree while a four legged serpent watched coiled around a branch, and still another with the same feller and his gal fleeing the forest, chased out by an angel with a burning sword.

Merely and another servant spread wide a set of double doors laced in gold, and gestured for me to enter. Giving them a long look and discreetly loosening the derringer in my sleeve, I walked in.

"Clay! There you are! I've been waiting for hours!"

"Maria, what're you doin' here?!"

"They said you were waiting for me, you'd meet me here."

Maria looked a bit uneasy, but she was unharmed.

"I been sleeping all day gal! What were you thinking?!"

"I was on my way to you at sundown, when one of those servants approached me, said you'd not wanted me to miss the big event, and had arranged for them to bring me to you."

"Couldn't you feel where I was?"

"Yes, one moment you were in the same direction where you'd gone to ground, the next I sensed you were on the ship where they said. This is all new to me Clay. Is this some trick?"

"I'm guessing so, but keep your voice down. These are the fellers what have been helping us the last few days, and they seem to be more in the know than you'd think about what's been goin' on here. I don't know what the angle is, but this is supposed to be some highfalutin' gamblers convention. Listen, we move fast and get off the boat, give them the slip, and-"

"Mr. and Mrs. Wilder! I am so pleased you could make it! I have been looking forward most earnestly to making your acquaintance!"

A man strode into the room. He wore an elegant suit, his beard well trimmed, but other than that he looked about just

like every fella I'd ever seen in my life, maybe in his late
forties. His eyes were a muddy brown, his hair the dullest
color of mud, tinged with grey; nothing about his features
was too large or too small. Only an odd scar on his forehead
stood out as memorable. He would have looked just at home
in overalls working the docks as he would in a governor's
mansion somewhere.

"I had to admit I was a little concerned you would not
arrive, we had been waiting for word of your plans to attend.
Please, I beg you, forgive the harmless diversion, it was
the only way I knew to ensure I would have the pleasure of
meeting you both!"

"A fella' what tries to trick you into meeting with him
isn't someone I can say I'm glad to know." I drawled, and
let the derringer drop into my hand behind my back.

"Ah, yes, well met good sir!" Icarus laughed, rich and
throaty, "I owe you an apology then. It's just that you have
gained some repute as a man of fortune, a player at cards,
and of course, the husband of a very special sort of bride.
Well, I see you are now similarly gifted! An unexpected, but
most welcome surprise."

My brows knit up. "You mean you know-"

"That you and your lovely wife are vampires? Yes, and
what vampires you are! I must say, your kind is exceedingly rare, vampires who have kept their innocence and their
souls! If only you knew how many there were who could
say that. Less than a handful. There are so many special
creatures that walk the earth! But enough, you are here for
a game, not a history lesson. Suffice it for me to say that all
of your fellow guests here tonight have similar...peculiarities.
Gifts of their own. I only say this so you won't feel threatened. I would like to foster an air of mutual appreciation and
respect in this regard, for the enjoyment of all. I hate for an
evening to be spoiled by the specter of mutual suspicion."

I tipped my hat.

"Nice meeting you, Icarus. My wife and I were just leaving. Enjoy your party."

Icarus snapped his fingers at the servants standing at the door and began to speak.

"No need," I growled, pulling the derringer, and pointing it right between his eyes, "We'll see ourselves out."

Icarus looked down the twin barrels and gave a soft chuckle.

"I really must warn against anything rash Mr. Wilder. I'm afraid it's quite impossible-"

"Not much is impossible, keep jawin' and we'll find out just what I can do."

I didn't know what he was about to tell me, but I didn't care. I didn't like the fact that he looked utterly unthreatened by, well, my threat, and a man that don't get nervous when you put a gun in his face is a man what's got one hell of a hole card.

I dragged Maria out of the room after me, just as I felt the ship moving, the steam engines chuffing as the wheels cranked up and started to spin.

One of the servants followed us.

"Please sir and madame, it is quite impossible for you to leave at the moment, we have already begun to depart-"

I shoved him away, he fell on his backside, and then we were running along the rail as the ship pulled away from the docks.

'We are going to have to jump!" Maria shouted over the noise of rushing water and engine.

"Let's do it then!" I stuffed the derringer in my pocket.

Maria and I climbed the railing, holding hands. The waters of the Mississippi rushed by, the steamboat was moving faster than any other I'd ever seen. I held my nose and we jumped.

I smacked my head against what felt like a pane of glass, Maria yelped in surprise as we was thrown back to the deck in a heap.

"Bravo, a most spirited attempt. It is, unfortunately, quite impossible for you to leave the game at this stage. No hard feelings, please. Allow me to offer you some refreshments, and you can meet the other guests."

Icarus walked through a set of doors, his two servants flanking them.

Maria bared her fangs, hissed.

"Careful darlin'. we're in up to our neck right now."

"Why couldn't we escape Clay? What is this place? Who is this man, and what does he want with us?"

"Sounds like he wants us to play cards. Whatever this is gal, we can't leave, though I ain't done tryin' neither. But there's something else at play here, and I aim to find out what. We'll play along, but be ready when I give the signal."

Maria threw up her hands in exasperation.

"Be ready to do what?"

I lit a smoke, breathed out a puff, "I'll let you know, just as soon as I do ."

CHAPTER 18

We walked into a large hall towards the front of the steamboat, the floor was covered in thick red carpet, huge glass chandeliers hung over the room, scattering the candle-light far and wide.

Men and women milled about, handling glasses of dark wine and nervously glancing around the room. A few were having whispered conversations.

I saw one face I recognized, staring at me with eyes cold and hard as ice. Ravenstone approached, glass in hand.

"What are you doing here?" He hissed at me.

"Same as you I guess, I'm here for the card game. Can't say as I had a whole lot of choice in the matter."

"This is no simple card game, you fool. Do you have any idea where you are?"

"I know I'm somewhere I didn't intend to be tonight, and as soon as I can, I'm leaving."

Ravenstone frowned. "You have more sense than I gave you credit for then, but in the end, not enough. No one can leave this ship once they've boarded. Spells most ancient and powerful will prevent that. Only the winner will leave this ship tonight."

"Just what kind of game is this? What's this Icarus fella want me here so bad for? I ain't got hardly a cent left to my name, and Maria doesn't know a whole heckuva lot about playin' cards. He's got no need to keep me around, unless he wants to stake me some chips, so I can take him for all he's worth."

I looked around at the lavish settings, Icarus could afford some losses.

Ravenstone leaned in, "Maria, if you did not wish to be here, I am very sorry. It is a pity for one so young as you to attend. Good form compels me to introduce myself. My name is Nathaniel Ravenstone, and I am pleased to make your acquaintance, though I deeply wish it were under better circumstances," He lifted Maria's hand to his lips. I'd have to keep an eye on this slick European feller, "I regret than I shan't know you long, nor your companion. Ah, I see the two of you are married, yes? All the greater sorrow then. For only one of you will survive, should you be even that fortunate. It would be best for you to lose early, I can only imagine how it will feel if one of you loses to the other."

I butted in, "What are you flappin' about? Maria isn't plannin' on playin' any cards, and I just told you I'm flat broke. I don't know what you mean about survivin', but the two of us have proved not so easy to dispose of, and we'll be moving along shortly, and perhaps a good deal richer to boot."

A gong sounded from somewhere, a great brass ringing that stopped all whispered conversation as Icarus grandly entered the room and stood behind a large circular table with his neatly manicured hands on the back of a chair.

"Ladies and gentlemen, it is my great honor and extreme pleasure to welcome you to the greatest gambling event of the century, indeed, the greatest you shall ever attend, though you all have years untold left before you. The winner shall have the prize that all of you seek, though there can be only one. The game will begin in a moment's time, and you will all have your chance to claim the prize you have chosen to risk all for. I sincerely wish every one of you good fortune, and whatever the outcome, know that your intrepid spirits receive due honor for the risks you have had the courage to take. This new world is being built in just such a spirit, and fed by the life of the very river we now traverse in this most modern of contraptions. For any refreshments you may require you have but to ask, we shall make every effort to supply your comfort.

Ladies and gentlemen, welcome to the Hades, the crown jewel of the Mississippi. My servants shall escort you to your tables. Let the games begin!"

I half expected the speech to end in the cheers of an excited crowd of gamblers, but the folks gathered in the great room just eyed each other nervously, or sipped at their drinks. There was about a dozen folks huddled about, and I wondered what was makin' 'em all so nervous. Must be a whole pile of money at stake.

Ravenstone turned to leave. I stepped after him and grabbed him by the shoulder.

"Wait! Just what in the blazes are all these folks so cowed by? I've beeves lined up for slaughter what didn't look this nervous!"

Nathaniel sighed, his eyes closed, "I thought you knew little before, and now I see you understand not at all your predicament. It isn't supposed to be done this way, as I understand the rules. We aren't playing for money! We are-"

"Mr. Ravenstone, I have been so looking forward to speaking with you. You are one of the eldest in attendance tonight. Such a cornucopia of the immortal, don't you think? Ones so young," he nodded towards Maria and me, "And ones so old. Come now, I'd be happy to escort you to your place at the table personally."

Nathaniel threw back the rest of his drink, and it was only then I realized it wasn't wine, but blood. Slowly, I looked around the room. Some of them were vampires, like Maria and I. Others had a different smell; their bodies were warm and practically throbbing with blood. There was another fella in a white suit with gold teeth and pocket watch and a rose stuck through his lapel that I couldn't quite make out. He looked like a real dapper riverboat gambler, beard as white as his suit and sparkling green eyes. Ravenstone was already following Icarus through the crowd to one of the tables servants were carrying into the room and covering in

144

green cloth.

"Right this way, Mr. and Mrs. Wilder." Merely appeared, and beckoned for me to follow.

"I ain't going nowhere! Get Icarus, Maria and I don't want to play your game."

"Oh sir, it is not my game, it is Mr. Icarus' game. The prize is quite desirable, all here have chosen to take the greatest of risks for a chance to obtain it. Truly though, there is no time for second thoughts, once aboard the Hades, there is no turning back. Perhaps you are in need of refreshment, might I offer you a glass of-"

In a blink, I had Merely by the throat, ready to crush the life out of him. I was only stopped by Maria, who suddenly put her hand on my shoulder.

"Clay, don't. Look." I followed Maria's eyes to seven vampires who entered the room in a flash, dressed as servants. Their faces were stone but they radiated menace nonetheless. Each one carried a large silver spear or an axe. The handles were decorated in miniature with folks appearing to be crawling and writhing in agony all down the handles.

I'd faced worse odds as a human against other humans, but my chances here didn't look so good, and crushing Merely's windpipe might provide a measure of satisfaction, but would do nothing to further Maria and I's escape. Might as well play cards, and meanwhile find a way to get the hell out of here. I was already broke, so I couldn't lose much.

"Mr. Wilder, I offer my gratitude for the life of my servant. It is good you chose not to execute him; I absolutely prohibit violence of any kind aboard the Hades. My servants here enforce that rule most...vigorously. Perhaps that seems a paradox. I am deeply sorry if he has offended you, might I soothe the sting by offering you a drink? Please, come and join us at the table, the other guests are waiting."

Merely looked like he was about to collapse, but handed Maria and I a crystal fluted glass filled with blood. I sniffed it but didn't drink. My appetite was gone.

We didn't have much choice. I followed Icarus to the table as Ravenstone had done and pulled out a chair for Maria. She didn't know cards very well; the few times she'd played she'd thrown our deck into the fire and said I was cheating. I was pretty much broke, we'd play a hand or two, and then leave. Hopefully by then I'd have figured a way out of here, even if we had to get through the vampire guards.

I gently pushed Maria's chair in and she put on a brave smile, though I could sense she was awful worried. I threw her a sly wink and sat at the table.

A servant came forward and placed an ornate wooden card box on the table.

I rubbed my hands together to remove the sweat.

"So what's this, poker? Who deals?" I asked.

As if in answer, the box flew open, and a hand popped out, holding a deck of cards. I didn't have much to say to that. It was just a hand, no arm or for that matter, body, attached.

The hand ran about the table on two fingers, deftly shucking cards around the table with its thumb. The other guests watched in wonder as the little hand dealt us each five cards. This was something you didn't see at any other riverboat on the Mississippi, or anywheres else, most-like.

"Ladies and gentlemen, please allow me to introduce Manus, or,"Icarus chuckled, "as my servants have taken to calling him, Manny. Some of you have not seen a disembodied hand before, or at least, not one so animated, but Manus is my oldest servant, and uniquely suited for his role in tonight's game. After all, it can truly be said, where there are no sleeves, there are not more than four aces to a deck."

Icarus looked rather pleased with his little speech. The other gamblers looked on in wonder. One shaggy looking fellow who looked more uncomfortable in a suit and tie than I did gave it a poke, but the hand flicked a finger back at him without losing control of the deck.

"Please, guests one and all, do not taunt the hand. This night is a tradition that only happens every century or so. The game is different in every era. In this time and place, we shall play poker. I trust you all are familiar with the rules?"

Icarus looked around. All of us nodded except Maria, who gave me a smouldering look. It wasn't my fault she was worse at cards than I was at bein' an honest man.

Servants entered the room in a line, encircling the table and laying down small stacks of chips, each of equal size, ten per player. The stacks all gave off a sudden faint bluish glow as they touched the cloth in front of each gambler. I felt strange when that happened, hollow inside.

"What gives? I didn't have to buy in? Asides, like I tried to tell you before, I'm durned near broke, so I hope we're playin' small bets, at least to start. Unless anyone cares to stake me?"

The rest of the gamblers looked at me in bewilderment. Ravenstone sighed. Icarus gave a cheery laugh, and then smiled at me.

"Why Mr. Wilder, we aren't playing for something so trivial as your American dollars. Aboard the Hades, we play for souls."

CHAPTER 19

Maria looked at me for guidance, but I didn't have much to give. If'n I thought we had a chance I would have tried to shoot my way out of there right there and then.

"Don't fret, Mrs. Wilder. Mr. Wilder, please do close your mouth. You see, everyone is willing to be here, and even though I admit to using a measure of subterfuge to ensure your attendance at my little game, I am only thinking of your benefit. You see, all the players at this table have the chance to obtain the thing which you all seek. All of us bear a curse in our own way. Each of you have sought long and hard for a method of dealing with it, of regaining a measure of your humanity, but each of you have failed in turn, time and again. Truly, only the desperate attend.

I offer a most accommodating solution to your plight. You cannot hope to defeat the curse on your own, but I can help. The demons who have bound in some way or another to your corporeal forms will always win; you have no chance of attaining freedom for the fate all of you must eventually succumb to, even should you walk the earth until the very end of time. Our two most uninformed guests here tonight, special cases though they may be, will eventually fall prey to their thirst. It is just a matter of time. The thirst always wins. For werewolves," Icarus nodded to the shaggy looking man and woman also seated at the table, "It is the hunger. The result is the same. Damnation. Each of you has a different picture of what that actually means, but only one here at this table truly knows, or should I say, remembers, the terrors it holds for you."

I cleared my throat. I didn't want to seem dense, but it was much more important to understand exactly what Maria and I was getting into here.

"So what's all that jabber mean then?" I went with the direct approach.

Icarus rolled his eyes, and sighed.

"Truly Mr. Wilder, I am most disappointed. It seems I have overestimated you."

It seemed I was destined to hear that I'd been estimated wrongly through the rest of my days. I was about to make a witty retort to that effect, but Icarus continued.

"We play for souls. The chips before you represent a part of each of your own immortal souls, though strictly speaking, they aren't so immortal in this instance, and that is where you benefit.

All of you face eternal torment, most of you have no idea how much of that you have already experienced," The vampires except Ravenstone looked confused at this point, "so your souls are truly only offering you an eternity of suffering untold. I take what can benefit you nothing, worse than useless, a detriment, and offer you something most precious in return, the chance for one lucky man or woman, one soul, to regain their humanity. The rest are used for my benefit. It will cause you no pain. Should you lose, you will simply cease to exist. Those of you who have chosen to come here and participate tonight have seen the benefit in that. Annihilation is preferable to damnation."

"So what'dya use the souls for? I figure a feller's got a right to know."

Icarus steepled his hands under his chin. His muddy eyes twinkled.

"Very well, why not? Most of you shall cease to exist after the game, the victor, well...the victor will find the following information absolutely useless to him after he is... restored to his proper state."

Maria gave me a look then, like there was something I

should pick up on there, but I didn't pick up the trail she was layin' for me. Icarus continued.

"Many, many years ago, I found myself a castaway, abandoned by man and God, as you also find yourselves to be. I would have lived much longer than a mortal life, but one found me, rescued me from my exile, became a mother to me. Many of you here tonight are connected to her in some way, but I will say no more of that. I built a great city, and with my surrogate mother, more loyal to me than my birth mother, teaching me the deep magicks of the earth, I found a way to consume the souls of men. These did not last long, they burned too hot and too quick, and I searched for a more effective remedy to my mortal condition. The one who took me in offered up to me her own children for sustenance, so loyal was she to me, and I was able to consume souls which lasted far longer than any mere mortal. The souls of her children were bound to their bodies, they would have had thousands upon thousands of years upon the earth, and these proved far more nourishing. The effect was most beneficial, both to myself and the rest of mankind. I needed to consume far less lives, and the souls of her children would have shared a similar fate to your own. She viewed it as a kindness.

I also discovered, quite by accident, a means to restore one so cursed to their natural state or mortality, and so freed from the curse they were able to seek out redemption from God. Such has never been my way, but then, I exist on the souls of others, my own long since consumed by the very power that burns within me, I need not fear the judgment of God nor man. I have encased the power I speak of within an artifact, and the winner of this game shall have the chance to avail themselves of it. Lest you think to seize it by force I assure you it is most impossible to affect such a course of action. You have seen my guards, and I also have taken other, much more strenuous precautions. And now, since we have finished our little history lesson, and all are clear as to what is at stake, shall we begin?"

I felt a little out of my depth with this whole thing, but I slapped the reins and dug in the spurs anyhow. Maria beat me to it.

"Where are your chips?" Maria asked, her eyes aflame with barely controlled rage.

"Ah, a fair question Mrs. Wilder. I see you are more perceptive than your husband. Perhaps you shall outlive him, at least for a while. I do not play, of course. I assure, you, it would only serve to ensure that none of you had the chance to win your mortality. I have been gambling since the very dawn of the age, and playing power since it was called As Nas in Persia, and none of you are like to emerge victorious from a contest with me. When only one gambler remains, I shall accept the chips from him in exchange for the return of his humanity, or hers, if you prefer, and he or she shall be free to go, unmolested. Does that satisfy your curiosity?"

Maria didn't answer.

"Very well then, pick up your cards. The game is draw poker. The ante is one tenth of your soul. Please excuse me, I often forget how anxious this game can be for the participants. One chip, into the pot, if you please."

I hesitated for a moment, then tossed it in. A hell of a thing to throw into a game of poker. I had to put such thoughts aside, and focus on the task at hand. Maria's hands trembled, and she threw one in.

There had to be a way out of this, but there was none I could find so far. There was no way to really win this, even with all the luck in the world. If there could be only one winner, there was no doubt in my mind that it had to be Maria. I'd give my all for that gal, up to and including my soul. Far better would it be to not lose either, but if I ended up having to choose, there it was. If'n I couldn't find us a way out of this mess, I'd have to make sure Maria stayed in the game long enough for me to see her to the finish. Bein' that she hardly knew an ace from an eight, that might prove a bit of a chore.

Icarus smiled at Maria.

"They say luck is a lady, so perhaps Mrs. Wilder will open the action for us."

Maria glared at her cards, but it didn't look like they were telling her what to do. She looked up, eyes full of uncertainty, and something else. Fear.

"Fold." She laid her cards face down.

I gritted my teeth and kept my tongue between them. This was not the way to win.

The Werewolf to her left grinned. "Bet. Two." He threw two chips into the pot.

"Very good Mr. Thresher, an aggressive start!"

The players mostly raised, only the old gambler in the white suit folded. I had three Aces right off the bat, and I saw the bets and drew two cards, which didn't help.

We threw down. The female werewolf took the hand, with a four of a kind. In twos.

She smiled like a wolf and drew in the chips, casting a vicious glance at Maria.

The next hand I was sitting on a full house after trading in two cards. A sharp looking vampire had surprised everyone when he pushed his chips into the pot. He tossed his head, throwing long blonde hair back over one shoulder, trying to look confident. He wanted to win big and fast, but I had a hunch he was bluffing. In my time on the riverboats and saloons along the Mississippi, I ran into all kinds of gamblers. Many relied on sheer luck of the draw, and usually ended up the poorer. Others made of it a game of sums and odds, knowing what chances they had depending on what they had drawn. There was more than a few who'd trained themselves to remember every card they saw played, and worked things out in their head as to how each hand would play out. I figured it was harder to read the cards than it was the men at the table, and so I took some time to learn how to study a man's movements and expressions. Most thought they had a real "poker face", and most didn't. Just the stillness of a man's features as he suddenly tried to not show a thing about his hand could tell you volumes, and exaggerated confidence was either a bluff, or a very clever way to make a body think you was bluffing. I'd caught a glimpse of Maria's hand, and bothering me even more than the fact that she wasn't guarding her cards was the fact that she held two low pair, fives and threes. She'd matched the bet made again by Thresher, and she'd be four down if she folded now. Even if the blonde vampire was bluffing, he probably had a better hand than she did. We'd need every chip we could pick up.

Even if we were literally playing to survive, this was the highest stakes game, and by its very nature would favor the aggressive. With full knowledge I was risking the fate of my soul on a half decent hand, I pushed my chips into the pot. Everyone else folded.

The vamp across the table swallowed hard.

"Gentlemen," Icarus intoned, his voice crackling with excitement, "Let's see your cards."

I slapped my cards down on the table, Maria trembled, waiting for the other vamp to lay down his hand.

The blond vampire's fingers trembled, his eyes went blank as the cards fluttered to the green cloth.

Three kings.

He looked around the table in a panic, pleading with his eyes. Icarus clapped his hands together and barked out a laugh.

The blonde's cheeks began to sink in; his eyes retracted into his skull, his flesh seemed to wither on his bones. His jaw fell open and he tumbled from the table, a husk. His soul was gone.

Icarus stood.

"And now, perhaps for a momentary recess. Refreshments are available at the bar, a most excellent vintage."

CHAPTER 20

Maria took my arm as we left the table.

"I don't know what I'm doing!" She hissed at me in a low voice.

"I already knew that darlin', but we got to learn you up right quick, or find a way out of here."

"And how's that coming?"

"Not so good," I sighed. "I think as long as we're in the game, we're safe for now. We'll split my chips, that'll buy us some time. You focus on survivin' unless you got a real good hand, I'll try and do the winnin' for both of us."

Maria nodded, "Lets split up. I'll take a look on the other side of the ship. You see if you can learn something that might help us get out of here. This is cruel. Only one of us can win. As far as we've been able to tell Clay, we're innocent, our souls in the same position as any other man or woman. We don't have to do this to avoid hell, this isn't how it's supposed to work. I'm not having my soul eaten by this man Clay, and I'm not letting him get yours either."

I drew her close, and kissed her forehead.

"Don't worry darlin', just focus on your cards. I'll think of somethin' directly."

She turned to go, then spun on her heel, faced me, "What-ever happens, we stand together, my love, don't you go try-ing to be a hero. This life would be nothing without you."

Maria went off in search of an escape route, and I took the other end of the ship. The werewolf called Thresher leaned against the railing, puffing a cigar.

"Saw what you did there, savin' your little lady..."

I turned, "What's it to you?"

He laughed, but it sounded like a growl, "Nothin', but take my advice, you cut her loose. Only one of us can make it. Sooner or later, that gal's nothin' but a meal. She'll drag you down."

Maybe it was just the tension, or maybe I'm just a touch prickly about my bride, but I yanked the derringer and shoved it against the werewolf's chest, snarling.

"I can't be hurt by bullets friend, they just sting a mite," he smirked at me.

"Yeah? What about silver bullets?" I asked, thumbing back the hammer.

His eyes went flat then.

"Mr. Wilder, I shall have to ask you yet again to refrain from violence aboard the Hades. Each of my guests represents something precious to me. If your body dies apart from the game, I'm afraid it's quite worthless to me, a waste."

Icarus was flanked by four of his vampire guards, their giant spears at the ready.

After a tense moment, I grinned and eased the hammer down.

"Thank you for your sense and discretion. I've had to warn you twice now Mr. Wilder, there won't be a third time. Now, if you please, fortune awaits."

We sat at the table, the disembodied hand skittered about, shucking cards this way and that. He might have no sleeves, but a hand that walks about all by its lonesome bears watching, regardless.

My start was bad; I met the ante, saw my cards, and folded.

Maria did the same. A vampire in a tuxedo swilled his glass of blood and laid down a royal flush. His fangs showed as he beamed from ear to ear. He made a joke about beginner's luck, but no one was in a laughing mood.

I played the next few hands conservatively, Maria and I had a windfall of chips from my early risk, and in the meantime the high roller in the white suit amassed a large pile of chips. Ravenstone was a step behind him. The she-wolf bet often and big, and lost the same way.

I'd just pulled a straight when I decided to start betting hard again. It had been good to back off after that early all-in. Just as I was studying the other players, the good ones would be studyin' me as well. I wasn't so foolish as to think I wouldn't have patterns or tells, particularly when all the gamblers at the table had the heightened senses of the super-natural. Hangin' back a bit after a fast start might throw them off a bit, or at least delay the process of them catching up.

I lost the hand and a small chunk of chips when the high roller slapped down a straight flush. A dark haired vampire was out then, she had no more chips to bet and couldn't fold. She had held a pair of sixes. The roller guffawed as her body shrunk and shriveled in her elegant gown. Servants carried her away. There was no recess.

The she wolf was running dangerously low on chips, but a pair of aces and eights got her back into the running with a daring bet. Maria's stack of chips was holding out so far, whenever anyone raised more than a chip or two, she folded. She only won two hands in the space of half an hour.

I drew four queens and stayed, Thresher looked like he was running a bluff. The high roller saw his raise of five chips, Thresher only held two in reserve. A solemn, gray haired vampire who had been playing conservatively saw as well, going all in to do so. It wasn't the best hand, but I raised three. The werewolf would have to go sooner or later and if I was honest, sooner was better than later. I didn't like his toothy grins whenever Maria lost a hand.

If he folded now he'd have to hope he got a winning hand above all the next round. If he had anything at all he needed to stay in and hope it was enough. Something seemed to bristle underneath his skin as he set his cards down. Fold.

It was time to lay down, I still had a reserve, but if I lost this hand it would set me back too close for comfort. Just as well, I wasn't feelin' all that comfortable anyway.

The elder vampire dropped his cards first. A full house, Tens and threes. He looked at the roller.

The man in the white suit smiled, his gold teeth glinting, and dropped a four of a kind on a table. Same as mine. Exceptin' his was jacks.

The elder closed his eyes, peacefully letting death take him. Guess he viewed it as a blessing. Somehow that chilled me more than the fear in the other's eyes.

I dropped my cards. When the high roller saw the queens, them gold teeth disappeared behind a frown, his icy green eyes looked bloody murder my way.

The hand shuffled the deck and dealt out the cards, Thresher looked nervous as he threw in his last two chips. The chances of him getting a winning hand were small, he'd be all in so he could stay, but he wasn't likely to take the pot with this hand. This was his last stand.

He couldn't bluff, he had nothing to raise. So when his eyes went hollow and his chest sank I knew he had a bad hand. I loosened my own ace in the hole and made sure it was near to hand, two silver bullets in the chamber. At least those assassin priests had been good for something.

Thresher looked less and less in control as the betting ensued, raise three, raise five, two all-ins. At least two more players would be gone when the cards hit the table. Ravenstone was going head to head with the Vampire in the tuxedo. I'd taken to thinking of him as the Joker, since we hadn't spent much time getting to know names. I figured that was just as well.

Thresher was in it to the finish, but I didn't like his chances. He just kept glaring at the hand what had dealt him the cards. The Joker was the first to lay down, throwing four aces with that bright smile of his.

Before Ravencroft could lay down his hand, Thresher pounded his fist on the table, the disembodied hand scrabbling to the side just in time. Thresher tried for him again, missed. The hand skittered right off the table just as one of the guards put a hand on Thresher's shoulder.

The shaggy man leapt from his chair, his body crackling as bones shifted and rearranged, his skin sprouted black bristly hair, his roar turned into a guttural growl.

The vampire guard what had grabbed him moved in with his spear, aiming for the heart. Thresher slapped the spear aside with one big paw, the silvered blade slid into his side instead. The werewolf howled in pain and rage, but grabbed hold of his attacker's head and in the blink of an eye wrenched it free in a shower of blood.

More guards appeared in a blur, surrounding the werewolf with spears at the ready. The werewolf seemed to shrink as fast as he'd grown, slowly sinking to his knees and changing back into a human.

Thresher, now human, collapsed. The spearmen moved in.

"Stop!" Icarus screamed, "He's no good to me dead, put him in his chair."

The vampires picked Thresher up and slammed him down in his chair, each holding him down in it.

Thresher's clothes were in tatters, his eyes burned with hate and pain.

"Come now, Mr. Thresher. You chose to play this game, it's time to see it through to the finish. Who knows? Perhaps Nathaniel here is sitting on a pair of twos. Highly unlikely I know, but you also know what awaits you in the afterlife. Werewolves have perhaps the hardest time controlling their passions. I know the things you've done under the fat, full moon, and you give fresh meaning to the term "beast". All those poor women," Icarus chuckled, "I shan't like to be you in a few moments, unless of course, you do the wise thing and choose oblivion."

Thresher raised his shaggy head, and of all people, he looked to Maria and grinned. My fingers slowly moved from the table to my derringer. Maria met his gaze, unflinching.

"You're gonna' look like me real soon little lady. See you on the other side."

"No, you won't." I growled. Thresher wouldn't see anything at all, if icarus told it true. I almost killed him myself right there, just so's he'd get what I'd no doubt he deserved.

Thresher took his final moments to glare at me, and threw down his cards.

His body shook and rattled, as if fighting with all its might to keep his soul from being torn from it.

His throat let out a long, mournful howl, which died away as he crumpled to the floor, just skin and bones.

"Mr. Ravenstone, I believe that makes it your turn." Icarus licked his lips.

We all stared, but none so intently as the Joker, sitting there without a trace of humor now as Ravenstone's cards hit the table. A straight flush, 9, 10, jack, queen, king. Ravenstone didn't bluff.

As the tuxedo and the skeleton inside hit the carpet with a dull thud, Merely and two other servants arrived, holding a large bowl and a tray of glasses.

Icarus clapped his hands, "I believe we'll call a break. Refreshments everyone!"

Maria looked at me, a panic in her eyes. The table was down to five.

Merely took a glass and began to pour.

"Blood Punch anyone?"

CHAPTER 21

"This stuff is terrible. I really hope this isn't the last thing I drink." Maria made a face, but took another sip anyway.

"I'm gonna' kill him," I whispered. It was a bad plan, but better than the one that at best, meant one of us dying. I wasn't thinking this Icarus fella lived for ages and ages by being easy to kill, but even if it meant my doom it would give Maria a chance, I wasn't going to allow myself to win this card game, and that's assuming I could. I had a nice stack of chips, and Maria had guarded hers jealously, I'd only taken a few big risks and they'd paid off. She would have enough chips and few enough opponents where luck might just see her through. She could be human again, and live a full life somewhere, far from the Mississippi. Whatever was left of the order of Saint Michael would have no cause to hunt her any longer.

"Clay, I don't think it will work. Look at all the guards. They were on the werewolf in a flash."

I leaned in to whisper in her ear, "You know as well as I that even a vampire ain't so fast as a bullet. They might get me after, but no matter. I'll take my chances with the man upstairs and hope he's in a forgiving mood. Better than having my soul sucked out for some feller's meal. When I make my move, you stay put, you hear me?"

"Clay, you were the one who told me we could beat anything together."

"I know darlin' and we can. But how we win this one, don't include me sticking around for the victory party. You stay alive, and I win too. That's all I want. Things go well, we see each other again someday. Most folks wonder if the afterlife is real, we get to know it is. You just promise me you'll be good, and don't forget about me now..."

A bloody tear ran down Maria's cheek.

"Clay, there's just no way I could possibly let-"

"Everyone! Your attention please! Five of you are left, each of you has my heartfelt congratulations on making it this far. May I propose a toast to our fellows who have fallen this night, daring to risk all for one chance at their heart's desire!"

Ugh. The punch was bad.

"Now, if you will take your seats, fortune awaits the victor. We shall play until only one is left standing. Ladies and gentlemen, good luck!"

Icarus was positively glowing with good humor. The Vampire guards surrounded the table with their long spears, they clearly weren't about to allow a repeat of Thresher's antics.

The hand thumbed out the cards, I took a deep breath and a peek at mine.

Aces and eights. Two pair. So much for luck.

Maria was distracted, no doubt thinking of my plan, but I needed her to focus on the cards. She let her hand drop a little, I could see it was no better than mine.

I folded, laying my cards down quite pointedly, and she got the message. Only Ravenstone, the high roller, and the she-wolf were left in the game. After her initial run, the gal had cooled off some when she'd lost big, and had been steadily growing her collection of chips while avoiding any further big losses. Ravenstone sat atop the biggest pile, and me and the man in the white suit was about even. When I took my shot at Icarus, I'd shove her my chips, and she'd have a pile equal to Ravenstone's. It was the best I could do for her. Heavens, let it be enough.

The she wolf needed to win big, she had the smallest pile, and the others could force her to go all in. From watching her bets and folds, I had a pretty good idea she was happy with her cards. You could almost see the wheels turning. She was aggressive by nature, only slowing down her betting when she had to lick her wounds some. The tension was getting to her; she was the kind that always wanted to be on the attack. I hadn't known there were werewolves before tonight, but I was getting the sense they weren't the type to bide their time.

The high roller raised ten chips.

She went all in, letting her confidence show. It was just as good to bluff the others into folding as it was to win the pot outright.

Ravenstone matched her bet without blinking an eye. The high roller folded.

Suddenly looking a little less confident, she tossed down a full house. Sevens and jacks.

Ravenstone paused, looking her in the eye, and laid another full house down on the table, nines and tens.

The she-wolf let out a long sigh of relief. Ravenstone had lost almost half his chips, but we was all sitting near even. Maria had the least chips, but that would change soon. I'd do it as everyone was laying down their cards. They'd be expecting movement, which might give me a heartbeat longer than if'n I suddenly burst into action. Icarus paced around the table, rubbing his palms together with excitement.

Manny the hand dealt again, and we picked up our cards, throwing the ante in as we did so.

Maria had excitement writ large on her face, she was finally sitting on a good hand. I just wish she hadn't showed it so plainly.

My own cards were just middlin' so I folded.

Ravenstone folded as well, but the she-wolf opened the betting with a fifteen chip raise. I smelled a bluff. She had won the last hand, but hadn't been near so sure as she should have been to go all in like that, and it had given her confidence.

High roller picked a speck of lint off his white suit and decided to stay in the game. I was awful nervous for Maria. She hadn't always picked the best times to bet tonight.

To my surprise, Maria pushed all her chips into the center of the table.

From the sudden twitch of panic in the she-wolf's left eye I knew she'd been straight up bluffing. Cursing in another language, and you could tell it was a curse by the sound of it, she folded, looking like she was fittin' to burst from the table like Thresher had done. A shudder ran through her body, but she kept it in control, the vampire guards had stepped in, their spears and axes raised high.

"Careful now Tanya, you don't want to let your instincts get the better of you," Icarus warned. Tanya kept her eyes on the table.

The high roller looked at Maria, tryin' to sense whether she was really holding good cards. They'd doubtless figured she wasn't so good at hiding her emotions, or at figuring the odds, what few times she'd taken a small risk, she'd lost twice as often as she'd won.

I panicked inside. Maria must really think she had a good hand. She was tryin' not to show she did, but she was givin' it all away. I hoped it was as good as she thought it was, but I was ready to try and shove more chips in front of her if she went bust, but I had no notion if it would work.

The high roller glumly folded, staring down at the green cloth.

Maria raked in the chips, pointedly giving me a peek at her cards as she did so.

And ace, high card. Nothin' else.

"Gal, you had me worried some," I said, leaning close, "But you're learnin'!"

CHAPTER 22

Maria folded the next hand, and I was glad. I didn't want her to get greedy. One player that had more experience but wasn't learnin' that lesson none too well was the she wolf.

I was sitting on two pair, and didn't draw any help. Tanya tossed a handful of chips in the pot, raising. The high roller went all in, with a second's hesitation. If he was bluffing, he would have tried to look a little more confident, or make a show of barley concealed unconcern. I knew that from watching him. He had tells, but they were subtle. I didn't figure he let anything out that he didn't intend to, and whenever I'd read his tells, it hadn't led anyone to win big. He was about to play someone for a sucker. It wouldn't be me.

Tanya glared at him, but her pot was low, and I could see from her scrutiny she was weighing whether he was bluffing. She had quick sharp eyes, and I didn't figure she'd failed to catch the split second where he appeared to waver before going all in.

Tanya thought for a moment, and matched. Ravenstone had folded.

They were head to head, and one of them wouldn't be there the next time a hand was dealt. You could have heard a pin drop. On the carpet.

Tanya took a deep breath, and threw down her cards like a challenge.

The high roller looked at her full house, and his face fell. His lower lip trembled slightly. Tanya broke into a wide grin. Just as the high roller began to laugh.

He dropped the act and straight flush, and burst into laughter. Tanya's eyes went wide in sudden horror, but her flesh was already withering as her soul was sucked away. The servants carried her off.

He had to win, that I knew, but he enjoyed being cruel.

Manny the hand dealt again before Tanya's shrunken remains had even left the room.

Maria folded right away, then Ravenstone. I bet ten, mostly to try and keep the roller from swamping me with a bluff while I waited to see if I could fill in the gut shot hand. All I needed was a queen of spades, and I'd have a royal flush. Any other queen and I'd have a straight just the same, but the odds were slim I'd pull it off, and if I didn't I'd have an ace high card to go with.

Somethin' in my gut was just tellin' me to go for it, and even thought I knew the worst thing a gambler can do is let his anger control his wagers, I drew a card and saw the roller do the same. One card. He was sittin' on something very similar to my hand.

I watched his face but it was stone. No sign of how he felt about the card he'd drew played on his features. I hoped there was nothing on mine either. For all I knew, I had no tells. But there's always something, if you knew how to look. I might not be able to read the roller, but I was willing to bet he could read me. If I tried to bluff a bluff it would be obvious, a little sign would tip him off that I didn't really have what I was tryin' to get him to think he figured out I had.

So all I did was think of how I'd feel if I had drawn a bad card, and let it show on my face.

I pushed my stack of chips into the middle. Maria gasped. I tried to keep a stone face, like I'd do if I didn't want him to see how worried I was.

The roller's eyes rolled over my face. He was searching for something. I couldn't show a tell now, I thought of how Michael's face looked before I'd hammered it to pieces, made of marble.

The roller sniffed, then shoved his chips into the pot. All

of them.

"Got you," He gloated.

I slowly looked up to meet his eyes, looking away then to Maria.

"Clay"!" her eyes widened in panic, and for a second I hated to do it.

Then I looked back at the high roller, grinning at me with them gold teeth and that white suit.

"Mr. Wilder, will you kindly show your hand?" Icarus said, electricity in his voice.

"Why sure!" I broke into a grin.

I laid the hand out in a flourish. Rare as hen's teeth, the royal flush in spades was reflected briefly in the roller's eyes as he looked on in disbelief. It didn't matter what he had.

He jumped back from the table with astonishing speed, and in the next breath was pointing a large gold plated pistol in every direction. The guards backed up a step, I stayed stock-still. It didn't look like no ordinary pistol.

Icarus approached, his hands spread apart.

"I'm afraid you really must sit and play your hand, old friend. I'm sorry things didn't work out for you, but a bet's a bet, now isn't it?"

"Hell with you Cain, I'm done with this! Let me off, or I blow you to kingdom come!"

Icarus didn't look one bit threatened.

"Now, now, you of all people should know this won't work. You know what this means," he said, pointing to the odd mark on his forehead.

"Hell with that too. How I know it even means any-thing?! I'm telling you, one step closer and I'll"

Icarus' face darkened then, and he took one deliberate step forward.

The roller cocked the pistol and fired, but Icarus didn't so much as blink.

The roller's body jerked, convulsed, crackled. The arm holding the pistol snapped, bone jutting out from his arm what was holding the golden pistol. His left leg was next. Then his whole body seemed to snap and close in upon itself, and then he jerked apart, burning to a crisp in midair. He barely had time to scream.

The mark on Icarus' forehead was glowing red, much like the stone had done on Michael's statue when it had reformed itself. Icarus picked up the pistol, examining it.

"A most curious artifact. A demon-killer. Exceedingly rare. A pity he didn't know what he was dealing with. And a wasted soul. I dare say he wishes he had played the hand he was dealt by now, or better still not to have fallen for your bluff. He was an old acquaintance," For but a moment, Icarus looked the tiny bit sad, or maybe he had something caught in his eye.

"Ah well, time moves on, old friends go, new friends come along and replace them. Deal the cards Manus, I shall add this to my collection."

Maria gave me a glance full of meaning, but she looked relieved. I had not fired at Icarus. It was a good thing too, whatever that mark was seemed darn sure to keep folks what recognized what it could do from trying to kill him.

It was down to me, Maria, and Ravenstone. And there could only be one winner.

CHAPTER 23

"What do we do now? Maria whispered in my ear.

I pushed my pile of chips towards Maria, "You bet enough to make him go all in, again and again, you've got enough chips there to do it to him at least twice before he catches up."

Maria stopped my hand.

"No, we do this together. We do everything together. I fold, you play. I'll hold enough to stake you in case you should go bust, and we just hope that works. But by the time you beat him Clay, you better have a better plan than your last."

"Thanks for the support darlin'," I said. In truth, she was giving me all the support I needed. She was trusting me to find a way out of this for us. And then it came to me, and it just might work.

"Ravenstone, we need to work together-" I started, but Ravenstone cut me off.

"That's not the way it works. Trust me, I've spent a lifetime looking for shortcuts. I'm very sorry for you both, especially since neither of you wanted to attend. But things being what they are, I'm in this to win. You've got more chips than I, and that bodes well for your chances, but I don't intend to make things easy for you. If I should fail, well, as I explained earlier, annihilation is far superior to eternal torment."

"What if it didn't have to be either? We don't want to beat you Nathaniel," Maria tried, "You can have the artfifact. Clay and I may have the bulk of the chips, but we can't win this without one of us losing. That we won't do. We'll be reduced to that either way if you lose this very next hand, so why not help us now?"

Ravenstone leaned his chin on his hand.

"I don't see another option. When you are in the game, you are in the game. I'm older and stronger than the other vampires here, but odds are odds, and they don't favor us. Being decapitated by a silver axe sends me to my greatest dread, losing the game is a sweet surrender, and winning gives me that which I desire most, a chance for redemption and an escape from hell. Why should I risk all when what I want is right before me?"

"Because you have a chance at something more. Help us, and you can have the artifact. I don't believe redemption depends on it. We had to deal with things the same as any human, or have you forgotten? Men and women have desires too, just as dark and just as evil as a thirst for blood. Being human won't change what you are, or what you've done. Why not try standing for your redemption right here, right now. You had to choose to become a vampire and forsake salvation; you had to choose to risk your soul in this game. It's about choices Ravenstone, make one, or you can sit and just let something happen to you."

Ravenstone didn't speak, just kind of set there a while, lost in thought.

Icarus entered the room.

"Well, lady, and gentlemen! Are we ready to finish the contest? I am most anxious to discover who shall be our victor!"

"You won't have one." Maria stood.

"Oh nonsense Mrs. Wilder, we always have a victor. Now please do sit down, you have wagers to make."

"No. We refuse to play, my husband and I will not finish your game."

I stood, catching on, "That's right. We just won't finish."

Icarus clapped his hands and burst into laughter.

"Bravo, Mr. and Mrs. Wilder, bravo! Now, really, please

169

do sit down, I'm afraid it's quite impossible to quit once you've started. I myself, can never get enough. I used to play in the games myself you know, though I have only watched for centuries."

"You deaf?" I growled, "We said we ain't a'gonna' play. You might as well just let us go now, and declare Ravenstone the victor."

Icarus stopped smiling.

"Oh dear, you really are serious. I do so hate to waste a soul, even more so two, and we have already lost one to begin with this night. Such a shame."

Icarus snapped his fingers. The vampire guards loomed closer, surrounding us with their great shining blades at the ready.

"Now, are you both sure about this? Just as you've heard me warn the others, my solution is much preferable to the alternative, a valuable service, if you will. Perhaps I should explain it agai-"

"No need," I interrupted. "We get the picture. The cursed go to hell, unless you swallow up their souls entirely. But Maria and me, we're different. neither of us chose this, not the way it's supposed to be done anyway, and near as we can tell, our souls are as clean as when we were humans, though my own's like as not a mite ragged around the edges. That bein' said, we aren't slated for damnation any more'n any one of them folks out there on the passin' boats."

Icarus stroked his short beard.

"A most interesting notion. Are you quite certain-"

"Maria and I ain't never fed on the innocent, and we ain't controlled by the demons folks say live in our blood. We may not be human, but we're a durned sight apart from your regular vamps. Which means our souls might just be somethin' special. Somethin' a critter like you ain't never had a chance at before..."

I let that last hang, Icarus would come to his own conclusion. He was a gambler, that's the form he chose to satisfy his hunger for the souls of mortal and immortal alike. I didn't know if this would work, but it he was the gambler I thought he was...

"Ah, a soul joined to an immortals body, trapped on this plane, yet uncorrupted. Such a soul, and better yet, two, could just...paradise, could it be?"

Icarus' eyes went all distant, like a buffalo hunter's. That's when I knew we had 'im. I didn't have the first notion as to whether any of this would work, but as long as he was thinkin' it just might...

"So," he was all business now, "What is your objection to continuing the game? You were doing well enough before, why stop now? You were in peril before, why refuse me at this hour?"

Maria piped up, "Clay and I refuse to play against each other. You can kill us if you wish, and we cannot leave, but you cannot force us to play. Nothing, nothing will cause us to destroy the other in this diabolic game!"

Icarus nodded. "So what do you propose?"

"You enter the game. Of your own free will. That should balance the odds. We have to finish, we finish. Ravenstone can keep goin' if he wants, or you let him drop out. If'n you get us, I don't think you'll be needin' him. One big pot, winner take all. We win, we both get our curse broken, human again."

Icarus thought for a moment, but the glint was in his eyes.

"Returned to the state you were in when you became vampires. Yes. Done. Now, let's play. I must say, this will be the most exciting game I've had in millennia, maybe ever!"

"Are you with me on this?" I asked Maria. It was a chance to be human again, and we weren't getting off this ship with Icarus alive, I had no doubts about that.

She looked me in the eye, nodded, and then kissed me, long and deep.

"I'm ready."

We sat at the table, Manus ran around on his fingers, dealing the cards.

"Tell me Icarus, why did that feller with the gold choppers call you "Cain"?"

Icarus smiled wanly, "I was beginning to think I had underestimated your cleverness Mr. Wilder. You have proved me wrong once again. He called me by that name because it is, after all, my name."

"Wait, so you're-"

"Yes, that one. From the book. Though I do like to point out, on the rare occasions I have the opportunity to discuss it at all, that I wasn't given the fairest possible treatment in the account, there was so much more to be said. All in all, I was made out to be quite the villain."

"Can't imagine where they got such a notion," I drawled, picking up my cards.

"Yes, well, it's to you Mr. Wilder, place your bet."

"I'm all in."

"Wouldn't you like to draw a card first?"

I grinned. "No need."

Icarus regarded me with one eyebrow arched.

"We're all in here Mr. WIlder, winner-take-all, remember? No need to bluff."

I locked eyes with Cain.

"I don't need to bluff."

CHAPTER 24

Cain, Maria, Ravenstone and I sat at the table, surrounded by the vampire guards. We were in this now, a chance to win our freedom from the curse in our blood, and if we failed, annihilation. I'd taken many a risk in my life, and plenty of gambles, but never with stakes like these.

Ravenstone, the fool, had stayed in the game. He still wanted what he came here for.

It wasn't just my life I was betting on, it was Maria's. She was depending on me to make this happen for us.

I picked up my cards, my face set like stone. Manus had dealt me a king, a queen, a jack, a ten, and a two. One card away from a royal flush. In spades. I'd just had that hand, the rarest hand in poker, and now I'd nearly gotten it again. Nearly.

Cain stared at me over his cards, his eyes twinkling. He liked his hand, and wasn't afraid to show it. Form the look in his muddy eyes, he hadn't had this much fun in years. For all the risk he was taking, his entire existence of thousands of years, Cain just could not resist the allure for one last gamble, the highest stakes he'd ever played for as well.

The first murderer the world ever knew clinked his stack of chips, just as large as a mountain before me, he contained so many souls within him.

"Well, Mr. Wilder, as much pleasure as this moment brings me, I am anxious to claim my prize."

"And so am I Cain, but I want to see it first. What is it we get if we win?"

Cain snapped his fingers, and the gong sounded again.

"I shall indulge you, but I fear you won't claim your

prize. It may only be used by one of you, the lure of a chance is enough to draw whom I seek, and I don't like to waste useful souls. Vampires and Werewolves seeking release from the curse are exceedingly rare, particularly in this day and age. So many of you are learning to embrace what you are, though I suppose it's just as fair to say they are equally ignorant of the consequences of their condition."

Two servants brought in a large brass urn, crudely worked, chips of some blue stone embedded in it. It looked old, beyond time.

"Mere mortal servants may handle it without effect of course, since its only purpose is to restore one cursed to their original state. They, as you can see, are most regular. But enough, let us begin."

Cain would lay first, by the order we'd been dealt, then Maria, then Ravenstone, then I.

I didn't know what Maria had, but I could not let her lay cards before I did. If her hand wasn't the winner...

Cain laid his cards down with a flourish, grinning ear to ear. Maria gasped. Ravenstone closed his eyes.

He had a straight flush. And there's only one hand that beats a straight flush. And I was one card short.

Maria looked at me, mouthed, "I love you," and began to lay down her cards.

I stopped her. It was time to take the gamble of a life-time. In more ways than one.

I laid the cards flat and spread them out with one hand.

"No! It's impossible! This can't be!"

Cain's eyes were wild as he stumbled back from the table, unwilling to believe his eyes.

He could not blink away the ten, jack, queen, king, and finally, the ace of spades.

"How did you...This can't be happening! MOTHER! HELP MEEEEEeeeeeeeeeeeeee...

Cain's frame bent and twisted as he shriveled and began to contract. Thick blue-green smoke bellowed from his mouth, nose, and ears. He knocked over the table with the punch on it, the glass bowl shattered on the floor.

Cain reached out for something in the sky, then his arm collapsed and one last hiss of smoke escaped his shriveled corpse.

You could feel the sudden inflow of air, as whatever Magicks bound the interior of the ship died with their maker.

Then all was still and silent, the only sound was that of the sidewheel churning the Mississippi.

Everyone was frozen, vampire guards and servants, Ravenstone and Maria, all staring at the withered husk that was the eater of souls.

Now was the time. I dashed to the nearest guard, and fired my derringer through his head. As his brains blew out the back of his skull, I snatched the axe from his hand and whirled, firing my second shot at the guard nearest Maria even as I brought the blade around to slice through another guard's neck.

By the time the vampire's head hit the floor, the rest of the guards were springing into action. Maria fetched up the spear from the guard I'd shot and used it to lop off his head. The remaining four guards sprang at us with a fury, but Ravenstone grabbed hold of the foremost spear and used it to lever its owner up and over, then buried the blade in its chest, pinning it to the floor.

He leapt aside the next moment as another guard charged him. Maria deftly ducked a thrown spear, and slashed at a charging vampire. I smashed another guard in the face with the butt end of the axe.

A vampire armed with an axe slashed at Maria from behind, she whirled and raised her spear just in time to partially block the blow; the blade grazed her neck, splitting the amulet I'd given her in two.

More guards poured into the room, which was awful disappointin' since I figured we were just about through.

The new guard spread out, holding spears and axes and

even short swords with thick blades. They closed around us. Maria, Nathaniel and I moved back-to-back, our weapons ready for the charge that would soon come.

One vampire edged forward, feinting with his short sword. Maria leapt forward snarling, shoving the point of the spear through his face and out the back of his neck. She flicked the spear, sending his body flying into the other guards. It would buy us a few seconds but no more, they'd come soon and all together.

KEE-WRAAAACK!

Everyone in the room looked up just as the roof exploded down on us. Everything disappeared in a shower of wood, plaster, and shattered chandeliers.

I sought out Maria's hand, and had to duck a sudden swipe from her spear when I found it.

"This way!" I backed up to one wall, waiting for the smoke to clear. The door to the outside was on the far side of the room.

The dust began to clear, carried away by the night breeze of the Mississippi, revealing a hulking figure kneeling in the middle of the room.

The figure rose, and bellowed.

"See me and despair, you unholy ones, for now you face the wrath of Michael!"

Maria and I looked at each other.

"I thought we killed him Clay!" My bride complained.

"I thought so too gal, but there he is."

Cain's vampire guards charged, but Michael cut through them like butter, his great stone wings acting as whirling blades, his huge hands grabbing and crushing vampires as he spun like a dervish through the room.

A vampire charged him with a spear, raking the marble with the tip, scraping small chunks of marble. The stone glowed and reformed, smoothing out the wound.

Another charged with an axe, sinking it deep into Michael's thigh.

"He's invincible!" Ravenstone ran to us, shouting. The two weapons that might have helped were wiles upriver in Memphis, we were too far away. I would have to make do. I cut a stumbling vampire in two when he got in my way and dragged Maria past the carnage, Ravenstone followed hot on our heels. Michael spotted us and roared, the sound like booming thunder over the waters.

He smashed through a section of wall like it was pasteboard, and stomped after us, shattering the deck with every footstep.

"We can't stop him!" Nathaniel screamed.

"I done it before, twice, I just need to find a way to make it keep better!"

Maria elbowed me hard in the ribs.

"We done it, alright? You happy gal?" I shouted over the rushing water from the sidewheel.

Michael launched himself into the air and landed in front of us, cutting off our retreat.

We turned and ran the other way. I...we may have beaten the huge stone statue into a pulp, but we didn't have the weapons we used to do it, and he was looking whole as ever.

We ducked in a side door, and Michael ducked through the wall. We raced up and down corridors. Michael smashed through wood and tile, undaunted. He wasn't going to let anything get in his way. I remembered something suddenly, and shoved Maria on ahead.

"Clay what are you doing?" Maria screamed after me as I turned around and ran straight at the raging statue.

"There's something I need, I'm gonna draw him off, you find that gold pistol! The demon-killer!"

"Where is it?" Maria and Nathaniel shouted together. Nathaniel was terrified; he'd nearly met his end at his former friend's big stone hands centuries ago.

"If'n I knew, I'd be a'runnin' that way! Just find it, and fast!"

Nathaniel grabbed Maria's arm and ran as I charged

Michael.

The huge face broke into a grin as he raised his big fists, preparing to smash me to smithereens.

At the last moment, I ducked and dove between Michael and the wall, and he tried to stop, the deck boards tearing up and skidding beneath his massive weight.

I ran up a flight of stairs and dodged up the next flight as a stone wing smashed through the wall where I'd been a half second ago. A disembodied hand skittered up the steps ahead of me as best it could, Manny. I snatched him up with me, carried him along.

I came to a dead end in a large bedroom with a collection of medieval weaponry on the wall. Michael charged into the room as I hefted a heavy sword off the wall and attacked, slashing the great sword like a club over Michael's outstretched wing. I ducked one of his fists, spun away, and snatched up a spiked ball and chain. Swinging it around, I hurled the heavy steel ball against Michael's chest, tearing off great hunks of stone. The spikes stuck fast in the stone and the weapon was ripped away. I searched around for my next weapon, and something prodded me in the leg. Manny the hand thrust a mace at me; I gripped it and swung, breaking a small chunk of a stone wing.

I fought hard with the weapons of knights and lords, but to no avail; any damage I did was either inconsequential or quickly glowed molten and repaired. I needed a way out of these close quarters, but Michael was between me and the door. If'n I hadn't been turned a vampire he would have crushed me minutes ago, as it was I was barely staying a step ahead.

Thinking quickly, I flattened myself against a wall, waiting for his charge. Manny climbed up my leg and dug himself in my shirt pocket, cowering. Michael didn't let me down, rushing at me headlong. At the last moment I dove out of the way, Michael's momentum carrying him through the wall like a charging buffalo. I grabbed a shield and a war hammer out of the case on the wall and leapt after him. I needed to keep him busy until Maria found what she was looking for.

Michael landed with a great crash on the deck in the midst of fleeing vampires. He grabbed one in his arms and ripped him in two, another he grabbed by the head and smashed into the deck face first. Smoke, ashes and cinders filled the air, the remains of slain vampires.

I came charging up to the terrible statue from behind, swinging the war hammer.

Michael turned, but a moment too late, and the big hammer smashed into his chest.

This was no Thorisen, and even though my blow smashed him to the ground, the wooden handle shattered, split into a dozen pieces. Michael swung a wing broadside at me; I raised the shield just in time. I flew back through a wall, making holes of my own now, and landed in a heap in the grand ballroom where we'd played cards for souls.

I struggled to pick myself up, even my newfound strength shaken by the ferocity of the blow. Michael was on me in an instant, leaping in the air and coming down with a heavy kick meant to crush me to a pulp.

I took the shield in both hands, slamming back against the force of his blow. The world exploded.

I lay dazed and broken, my bones and tissues quickly knitting up, but not fast enough. With every injury healed, my thirst burned brighter, how long could I keep this up? The shield lay broken in pieces all around me, I was defenseless.

Michael stomped into view, looming over me.

"It's time you faced judgment, Vampire..." he growled.

I coughed, spat out blood, "You think this gets you anything?"

"Of course. When I rid the world of your cursed kind, then I shall receive my reward. I shall have completed my penance."

My hands inched closer to a bent spear lying beside me, next to a pile of ash. Its owner didn't need it anymore. I might be about to die, but I wasn't going meekly.

"Your time is finished upon the earth, child of darkness," the great voice boomed.

I heard the crunching of small feet on glass.

"No, Jude, it's yours." Ravenstone's voice.

"Get away from him!" Maria screamed from somewhere behind me. I craned my neck around to see where they were.

Maria held a golden pistol, pointed at the marble angel.

"What is that?" Michael boomed. "Even your pagan weapons could not destroy me, last time we met. An angel cannot be destroyed."

"This doesn't fire normal bullets Jude," Nathaniel's voice was cold, no trace of warmth for his oldest friend.

"It's a demon-killer," Maria snarled, "And you are not an angel!"

Maria fired, the blast lit up the night sky in golden flame.

Michael staggered back a step, and looked down at the golden stub of bullet sticking out of his chest, just above the stomach.

He looked up, his molten eyes smouldering with righteous wrath.

He took a step forward, and then began to change. In mid-stride, the statue hardened, broke at the joints, and slowly crumbled to the deck. A black smoke with blue gray tendrils interwoven arose from the rubble.

"NOOOOOoooooo!" A disembodied voice screamed. The mingled spirit of Michael along with what I could only guess was a demon hovered for a moment, then sank downward through the torn deck, and disappeared. You could still hear the echoes of terrible screams.

Maria helped me to my feet. A pair of vampires raced into the room, weapons high.

Maria stared them down, pointing the demon-killer.

The vampires backed away, then dove over the side of the

ship.

"Where's Ravenstone?" Maria asked.

"The artifact!" We both shouted in unison, and ran for the table in the grand ballroom.

"Stay back!" Ravenstone warned, going for the bronze urn.

"Don't do it Ravenstone, we won that, fair and square. Maria saved you from Michael, we saved you from having your soul swallowed by Cain"

"I'm sorry Clay, Maria, but I'm going first. It might be able to be used again, but from what I've read about it, there can only be one curse removed in a century. I will be that one. I've waited too long.

"I'm warning you Nathaniel-"

"You're too late, I will be human again!" Ravenstone placed his hands on the urn, and a soft glow spread throughout the room.

The urn restored him to his former condition, just as Cain had promised. It took away the curse that had kept his corpse alive for centuries upon centuries. The life drained from his face, his tongue rotted from his mouth before he had the chance to scream. Only a fast decaying eye held a hint to the terror he must have felt as the life was sucked out of him.

I leaned on a broken staff, letting my body finish knitting itself back together again. Maria would never be human again. Neither would I. I had failed her.

"Hey, estupido, why so glum?" Maria smiled up at me, her raven locks against my chest.

"I'm sorry darlin' I-"

"Sssh! Nothing to be sorry about. We have each other right? In the end, that's all that matters. We'll deal with anything else as it comes."

"You're right darlin', there ain't much we can't do together, you'n me."

We just stood there for a moment, holding each other. I

closed my eyes, and let the breeze wash over us.

"Uh, Clay?"

"What is it darlin?"

"The sun is about to come up!"

"What?!" My eyes flew open. I grabbed Maria by the shoulders.

"Maria, where's your necklace?!"

"It got split in half in the fight! It fell off!"

I looked around, "We've got to find it, the sun will be over the horizon any second now!"

"What if we try for the ground?!" Too far away, no time.

"We'll never make it! Find that amulet!"

We scrambled through the wreckage. Light spilled over the horizon, stretching across the sky. I felt my skin begin to smoke, I might drop dead any second, out for the day. It would be a short sleep.

"Got it!" Maria shouted, lifting up a chunk of metal on a broken strap.

"That's only half, but put it on, it might work! I'll find you the other!"

"Here, you put it on Clay!" Maria tried to push the amulet on me.

I shoved her hands away, "We don't have time for this, take it."

I plunged into the wreckage. The sun started to break the horizon. I smelled burning flesh.

There! The other half glittered brightly in the light of the rising sun. I snatched it up.

I reached out to press it against the other half of Maria's amulet, but she grasped my hand in both of hers and pushed it down to my side, held it, and her mouth met mine.

The sun rose.

CHAPTER 25

We stood on the wreckage of the Hades, watching the sun rise high in the sky. For Maria it was magic, but I hadn't had much time to miss it. The amulet had worked somehow, we hadn't burst into flames, nor did we fall dead and helpless under the sun's rays.

There was no mistaking a sudden loss of our powers with the rising of the sun; half an amulet was too little it seemed, to maintain our full vampiric potency. It was almost like being human again, weaker, slower, but with less of a lust for blood. It would no doubt return at sunset, but at least the sun's light would not harm us, and we needn't be helpless in our graves, awaiting nightfall to live again, and our souls spending the days who-knows-where.

A small ship passed alongside us, throwing a line.

"What on earth happened here? This was "The Hades"? I heard tell of what a ship it was, but it don't look so fancy now, I gotta tell you. You folks all right?"

I grinned. I still felt battered and beaten, but my wounds had all healed.

"We're fine, just need a hand off this thing."

"Sure thing. Say, is that-"

"Gold plating? Yup. Take all you want. We just want to go to shore."

The captain of the tugboat grabbed a few chunks of loose gold tracery, and helped us aboard. He left the rest well enough alone.

The tugboat set a course for shore. It looked like Green-ville, we'd passed it a few times while Maria lay asleep in her coffin. She'd never have to do that again, she wouldn't have to miss out on anything that happened during the day.

"How did you pull out that second royal flush anyway? I thought the odds of something like that were near impossible..."

"That's 'cause it is darlin'. There was no way I'd draw the one card I needed to pull it off again."

"So how did you do it?" Maria arched an eyebrow.

I snapped my right hand open, and an ace popped into my hand from what was left of my sleeve.

"I cheated."

Maria laughed, "Only you would even try something like that."

"I didn't know it would work, I just had a hunch. Way I figured it, a body wouldn't think you could cheat at a game like that, and when folks don't think you can do somethin' that's when it's easiest to get away with it."

"You bet our souls on a hunch?"

"Well, when you say it like that-"

A sudden sound from the wreckage of the Hades caused Maria and I to spin around, fangs bared. Any surviving vampires should have been burned up when the sun rose, or they'd lie still and cold beneath the ruins.

A set of fingers stretched up over the side of a broken door, gripped it.

I was ready for anything.

Manus, or Manny the disembodied hand, skittered off the ship and up to the railing. Plucking a flower from the remnants of a vase, he drummed his little fingers along the side of the tugboat and held the daisy up to Maria.

Aw, he's kind of cute isn't he?" Maria bent down and plucked the flower out of the hand's, well, hand. There wasn't much else to him.

"Can we keep him?" Maria gave me her best pouty look, and I was powerless to resist.

"Fine, but you get to take care of him."

The hand waved, then started jabbing his finger, pointing

at something.

A metallic click behind us caused us to whirl. I wished for my derringer, or better yet, a brace of six-guns.

Familiar icy blue eyes gazed at us over four barrels.

"I tracked you, found your grave. You had escaped me again it seemed. But I found your weapons. Pagan names though they have, it is perhaps fitting that they will dispose of damned souls such as yours."

The cherub priest smiled. He'd been hiding aboard the tugboat, I didn't know if he knew his statue was nothing but lifeless rubble. He held Thorisdottir on me, the giant hammer was strapped to his back.

I wasn't feeling so fast, or so strong, and neither was Maria. The sun had drained us. But this time we faced a mere human, together.

"There's one thing you haven't thought of," I growled, striding towards him.

He pulled the trigger. Click.

I grabbed the barrels of the rifle, tore it from his grasp.

"You're real keen on blades, but even you should have had the sense to check the gun. It can't be reloaded, at least, no one still living knows how to do it."

I slugged him hard across the jaw. The priest spun away, and it was just a glancing blow. He was fast, and I was weakened by the sun.

He pulled a Colt peacemaker from his frocked coat, but I slapped it away from him as he raised it. He dodged as I tried to grab him.

He came back around, this time holding the hammer. I'd seen what it could do, and held the rifle up just in time to block the blow.

Thorisdottir shattered into a thousand pieces; I was thrown back to the deck. Maria leapt for the priest. He swung the hammer, she ducked, but the hammer smashed into the wall next to her, and the roof of the wheelhouse collapsed on her the next instant.

"Clay, I'm trapped!"

The priest smiled, and lifted the hammer high.

"No!" I screamed, and threw myself at him.

He turned, bringing the hammer around. This time, he was too slow.

I ducked under the swing, and grabbed his coat and spun him around. His own momentum carried him forward, all I'd done was give him a little push. He was quick, and got a foot up in time to keep from going over the side.

He swung, and I leaped back as the hammer whistled through the air. The hammer weighed a ton, but in your hand it felt light as a feather.

A shot rang out, and I flinched, expecting a bullet to rip into me.

The priest staggered backward, a red splotch widening on his chest.

The hull of the tugboat tripped him up, and he fell in the water with a great splash. He tried to swim, but the hammer only felt light to the person what carried it. It was strapped across his back, and in the water the massive hammer weighed as much as it should have, and perhaps then some. The priest struggled with the strap, but he was sinking fast.

He disappeared into the murky waters of the Mississippi. I didn't figure we'd be seeing him again.

I turned to see where the shot had come from. Manny the hand held the smoking peacemaker.

He spun the gun, and set it down. He fanned the smoke away with his fingers, but the effect was lacking.

He walked over to me, crawling on his fingers, and flipped over, offering me his palm.

I took his...hand, and shook him.

I helped Maria out of the rubble, and the hand picked up a few pieces here and there that he could manage. He couldn't toss them very far.

"Clay, do you see that?" Maria asked, shielding her eyes from the sun as she looked at the shoreline.

I squinted. The sun sure was brighter than I remembered, and that wasn't so long ago.

A wagon, painted black, with three men in it watched us pass from the shoreline. One of the men held a spyglass. On the other side were two more men, riders, at least one lens reflecting the rising sun. The order. Whose order it was now was anybody's guess, but they could pick whoever they chose, I reckoned. It wouldn't help them none.

The men in the wagon snapped the reins, and rode off. But they'd be out there, somewhere.

"They're still out there, still hunting us. Oh Clay, won't it ever stop?" Maria watched them, watching us.

"It stops right now darlin', 'cause now, we're huntin' them."

The End.

Colin Webster is a former U.S. Marine with plenty of experience in life or death situations and combat with firearms. He is intimately familiar with the weapons and armaments of the late 1800s. Colin has published *Blood and Silver and Blood and Tequila*. Colin lives in New Bern, North Carolina, where he works as an independent security consultant.